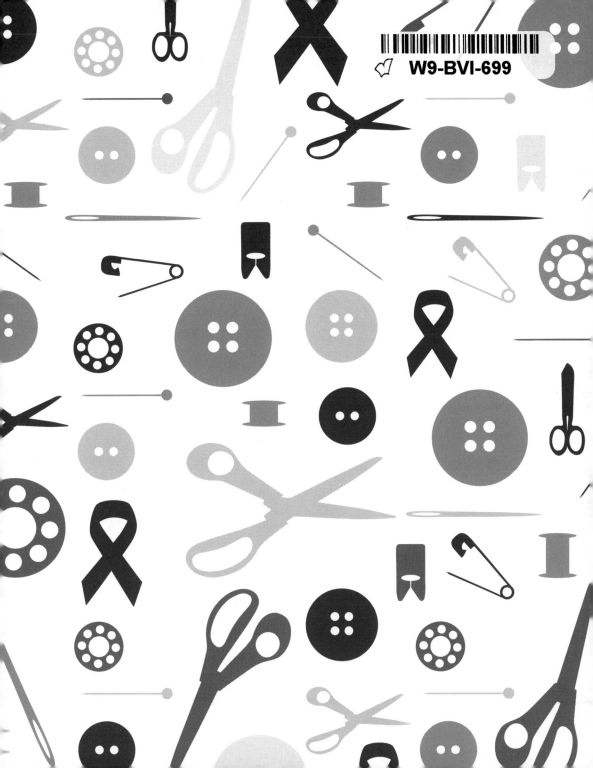

W9-BVI-699

# A Kids' Power Book!

Books inspired by real stories of young people who have taken action to make their world a better place

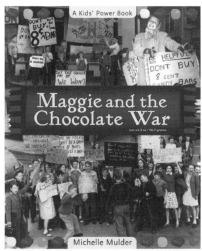

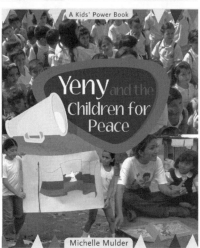

Praise for *Maggie and the Chocolate War*

"A great bridge between picture books and novels for early readers — highly recommended for community library kids' historical fiction collections."
    —*Children's Bookwatch, Midwest Book Review*

"*Maggie and the Chocolate War* connects readers to a time in history when a small group of children stood up for themselves and empowered other kids across the nation."
    —*Canadian Bookseller Magazine*

Praise for *Yeny and the Children for Peace*

"Tells the story of young Yeny and her protests against Colombia's history and high occurrence of violent acts."
    —*Children's Bookwatch*

"Highly readable in style, authentic in detail and tough to put down."
    —*CM Magazine*

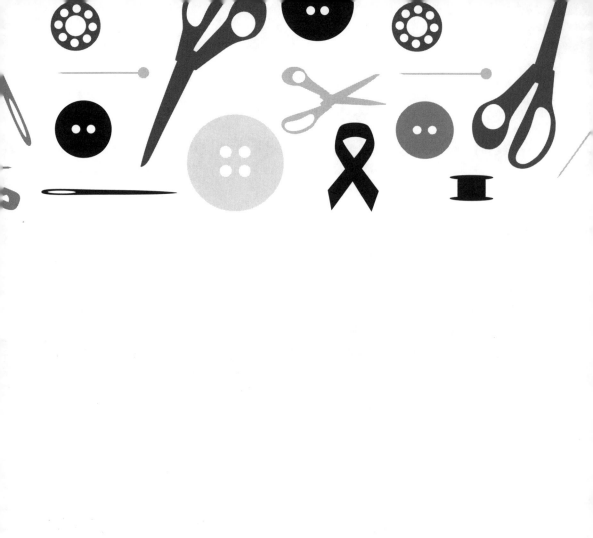

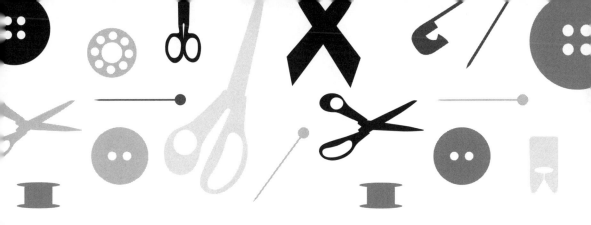

A Kids' Power Book

# Lacey *and the*
# African Grandmothers

Sue Farrell Holler

Second Story Press

LIBRARY AND ARCHIVES CANADA CATALOGUING IN PUBLICATION

Holler, Sue Farrell, 1962-
Lacey and the African grandmothers / by Sue Farrell Holler.

(The kids' power series)
ISBN 978-1-897187-61-6

1. Siksika Indians—Juvenile fiction. 2. Grandmothers to Grandmothers
Campaign—Juvenile fiction. I. Title. II. Series: Kids' power series

PS8615.O437L32 2009          jC813'.6          C2009-904794-2

Edited by Gena K. Gorrell
Copyedited by Karen Helm
Cover and text design by Melissa Kaita

Printed and bound in Canada

Photos courtesy of Sequoia Outreach School
Photos on page 23 and page 48 courtesy Sue Farrell Holler
Cover photos © istockphoto
Cover photo of grandmothers courtesy of Sequoia Outreach School

*Second Story Press gratefully acknowledges the support of the Ontario Arts Council
and the Canada Council for the Arts for our publishing program. We acknowledge the
financial support of the Government of Canada through the Book
Publishing Industry Development Program.*

ONTARIO ARTS COUNCIL
CONSEIL DES ARTS DE L'ONTARIO

Canada Council    Conseil des Arts
for the Arts      du Canada

Published by
SECOND STORY PRESS
20 Maud Street, Suite 401
Toronto, Ontario, Canada
M5V 2M5
www.secondstorypress.ca

To Lisa Jo Sun Walk, with thanks for allowing
me to tell your story, and to Denise Peterson,
who first shared this story with me.

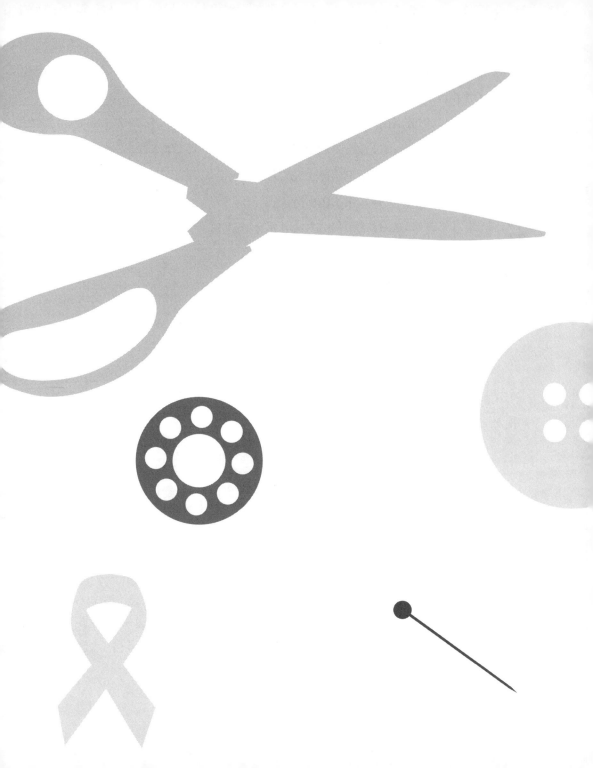

# Contents

*"We can do no great things,
only small things with great love."*
*—Mother Teresa*

# Author's Note

*Lacey and the African Grandmothers* is a work of fiction inspired by a remarkable young woman who was not afraid to use her talents to help others. Her real name is Lisa Jo Sun Walk.

The setting is real, as are the Sequoia Outreach School, Central Bow Valley School, and Blackfoot Crossing. The account of the African grandmothers visiting Lisa Jo and Sequoia is real, as is their visit to Blackfoot Crossing. Much of the conversation between the African women and Lisa Jo is based on their words.

It is my hope that readers will look at their personal talents and find ways to make the world a better place, whether in their families, their communities, their country, or, like Lisa Jo, in another part of the world.

# Preface

My name is Lacey Little Bird. I am twelve years old, and I am Blackfoot. The Blackfoot are part of the First Nations – the people who lived in North America long before the Europeans came.

My family stays at the Siksika First Nation, the second-biggest reserve in Canada, on the prairie in the middle of Alberta. Most of the land here looks as flat as a table, but it is really made up of gentle rolling hills covered with grasses and other plants. In the olden days our ancestors hunted buffalo here, and they could see the buffalo coming from far away. Now you can't see buffalo, but you can see the houses of the reserve.

At a place called South Camp, the prairie dips into a coulee. That's something like a valley, or a canyon. The Bow River winds through the bottom of the coulee, and along the river there are great trees with green leaves in the spring and summer. Berries grow here, especially *ookonooki* – saskatoon berries – the berries I like best. Other people call this place Blackfoot Crossing because of the new historical center there and because it was there that Chief Crowfoot signed a peace treaty in the 1800s, but we usually just call it South Camp. It is the part of the reserve where my family stays.

South Camp is a long way from the main part of the Siksika First Nation. A highway connects the two parts – South Camp

Above: The Siksika Nation is home to about 7,000 people. It is located just east of Calgary, Alberta. Below: A view of South Camp, taken from the marker that commemorates the signing of Treaty 7.

and the larger part that's beside Gleichen. The highway runs all the way to the big city of Calgary, which is about an hour away by car. Most families here don't have cars, so they don't leave the reserve very often.

I don't know why they would want to leave anyway. Siksika is the most beautiful place in the world. Sweet grass grows here, and sage, which smells so clean when you brush up against it. But the very best part is the sky. It looks like the inside of a bowl that's turned upside down. The sky is much bigger than the land. In the winter, when the sun is waking up, it paints the sky soft blue and pink. In the summer, when the sun goes to sleep beyond the horizon, it streaks the sky dark with orange and pink.

I'm going to tell you a story about Siksika, and about me. I'm just an ordinary girl with a mother, a father, a sister, and too many brothers. The story is about how someone like me got to meet grandmothers who came all the way from Africa.

The story starts with some seeds that looked like curled-up brains.

*Chapter 1*

# Planting Curled-up Brains

The smell of simmering herbs made my stomach rumble as I jumped down the stairs to Sequoia. I shook off the winter jacket I'd gotten for Christmas and slowed down when I hit the bottom step. I had run all the way from my own school, but running inside a school wasn't allowed, even in this school, which was in a church basement.

It was unusually quiet. No one was talking, and there wasn't any music. There were calculators, pencils, and erasers scattered on the long tables, and no one was smiling or joking. They all looked serious as they worked out the answers on the tests. I'd forgotten about the exams.

I crossed the classroom to the kitchen as quietly as an

antelope grazing. Lila, who worked as a secretary at Sequoia and liked to feed people, was slowly stirring a large pot on top of the stove. The steam made the kitchen warm and the air smell delicious. It also made Lila's face all shiny.

"It smells good in here. What are you making?" I whispered, popping a circle of carrot into my mouth and keeping another one in my hand. Lila doesn't seem to mind if I sneak carrot slices sometimes.

"It's beef minestrone soup. It has beef and beans and lots of vegetables. It tastes good, and it's good for you, especially if you are studying for exams," she whispered back. She stressed the word "exams" and held her finger to her lips to signal me to be silent.

I finished chewing and watched her dump carrots into the pot. "Are all the babies sleeping?" She nodded.

In total, there are more than seven thousand Blackfoot at Siksika First Nation, mostly kids. Siksika has three schools now, but I go to school outside of the reserve in a very small place called Gleichen. Gleichen has only about 450 people who stay there, but it has two schools. The best school, Sequoia, is an "outreach" school. It's for teenagers who have dropped out of school, sometimes because they have children of their own. My sister, Angel, goes to Sequoia.

When my school finishes, I usually head to Sequoia to look

after the babies so the parents can study, although it's really the parents' responsibility to look after their kids, even when they're at school. I love to look after babies, and I love being in the kitchen with Lila and watching how her arms jiggle when she shapes dough into biscuits or stirs a pot of soup. I also like eating the things she makes and sampling ingredients when she isn't looking. It's better than being at home, where there is hardly ever any extra food. Eleven people live in my house if you count Angel's baby, and eleven people eat a lot of food. Dad says we could eat a vanload of food every week if he could afford it. Sometimes we do eat that much, and then there is only enough money to buy things like noodles and peanut butter until Dad gets another job playing music at a wedding or a party.

"OK. Time's up. Pencils down." Mrs. Buchanan, the principal, stood up from her desk and spoke loudly. "Time to hand them in."

No one looked happy. They scraped their chairs on the floor, gathered their tests, and slumped to her desk, one by one, to give them to her.

"That was a biter. Guess I'll be starting math over again next week," groaned Kelvin as he handed her his papers. I was secretly happy that Kelvin might fail. He was the one person I truly hated.

"Maybe you'll surprise yourself. It could be a pass, you

know," suggested Mrs. Buchanan as she gathered the papers together.

"No way," he said. "I'm better at failing than passing." He slow-walked to the stairs, swishing his glossy hair and trying to look cool. Kelvin is my sister's boyfriend. He is two years older than Angel but, like her, he's in grade 11. I wish he would go away and never come back, the way his father had, maybe disappear somewhere in the city. There is nothing good about Kelvin except that he can fix things, like the amp for Dad's guitar, or my uncle's old van.

Kelvin likes cars best, though, especially shiny, fast cars. He likes them so much that he stole one so he could go to the city. That one wasn't shiny or fast, more like rusty and slow. But he took it anyway, even though it wasn't his and he didn't have permission. He got in trouble with the police for that, and now he has a criminal record. But the worst thing about Kelvin is the way he treats Angel, my seventeen-year-old sister. He treats her as if she is as dopey as a rock. He makes her feel small and stupid and worthless. I can't understand why she likes him so much.

I guess it's because of his looks. Kelvin is long and lean and has beautiful hair that falls over his eyes to hide what he is thinking. He likes to move his head in a slow circle, then jerk it to toss the hair from his face. You can see his eyes when he does that – angry eyes. He always seems as angry as a buffalo charging across the prairie to fight another buffalo. But today he looks like a troubled buffalo. Passing math is important to him. If he doesn't pass math, he can't reach his dream of becoming a mechanic. Still, I don't care.

As soon as they handed in their papers, the students scattered. Some went outside to hang out, some went to the bathroom, some went to check their babies, and some stayed to talk. Angel came into the kitchen.

"How was your exam?" I asked. She had studied nearly every night for two weeks. She needs to pass math, too, in order to get into college for nursing. I really want Angel to pass. She would make such a good nurse.

"It was hard, but I think I did OK," she said, pouring a glass of milk. She lifted her head to breathe in the steam from the soup. "Smells good. What's cooking?" she asked Lila.

"Beef minestrone soup. It will be ready soon. I thought I better feed those tired brains by filling you up with beans and noodles." Lila chuckled, then added, "Of course, most of you are already full of beans."

When Angel left to check on her baby daughter, Kayden, I noticed two big square bags piled up beside the counter that separated the kitchen from the classroom, and some trays with little compartments and plastic covers. They hadn't been there yesterday.

"What are those things for?" I asked, and slipped the second piece of carrot into my mouth.

"We're going to plant seeds and grow pots of flowers to make Gleichen look better," said Lila.

I lifted my eyebrows way above my glasses. "No one plants flowers here. That's for rich people in the city," I said. "Besides, someone would wreck them. Remember how they put nice benches outside the post office, and they were spray-painted with bad words almost the next day?"

"Yes, and remember how students from Sequoia repainted them to cover up the ugly words?"

"Yeah, and remember how no one liked doing it? Besides, it wouldn't be so easy to fix flowers," I said. "There would be broken pots and dirt everywhere. Gleichen would look uglier with all that mess."

"Maybe the flowers wouldn't be wrecked. But if they were, couldn't you just clean the mess and start over?" I thought Lila had lost her mind. Repainting benches was one thing, but putting flowers back together?

Lila must have guessed what I was thinking, because she said, "Right now, if someone came in here and dumped this pot of soup down the drain, do you know what I would do?"

I shook my head, but I had a pretty good idea what was coming.

"I'd start peeling more vegetables and getting another pot of soup ready. And do you know why?"

I shook my head again.

"Because soup is important. It feeds hungry people, and it makes them feel better. And sometimes the hunger people have isn't just for food. Sometimes you have to feed people by letting them see beautiful things." She stopped talking for a few seconds while she ran water in the sink to wash the cutting board and the knife. "So what would we do if someone wrecked all the flowers and broke the pots? Would we give up and let the badness win? Or would we keep giving goodness until the badness gave up?"

"We'd keep planting, I guess," I said, as I slid off the stool. "But I'm glad I don't have to do it."

"Ahem, *Lacey*," Lila said loudly. I wasn't far enough away to pretend I hadn't heard her. "Mrs. B. and I thought you could take on the project. The older kids can help the young ones get the trays ready and plant the seeds, but she wants you to take care of the seedlings. They have to be watered every day, and the students here are just too busy to remember."

I can't believe what she is saying. She wants me to waste my time growing plants and putting them in flowerpots so people could destroy them. "That's not fair," I said. "This isn't even my school."

"No, it's not your school," said Lila, "but you are part of the community. It is your obligation to help when help is needed." Her eyes and voice tell me she is serious.

I looked again at those bags and trays leaning near the kitchen counter, and I groaned. I knew they would make me do it.

Gleichen is so small that it's not really a town, but it has a grocery store, a gas station, a post office, a library, and a funny little park near the old water tower where there is a buffalo statue. It's hard to see the statue because someone planted big spruce trees there. When you are driving into town, you see the park and a big sign that says, "Glorious Past, Greater Future." The sign is talking about Gleichen, but I think it speaks about everyone. We can all have great futures if we want.

On the corner of the main street is a small white church called the Gleichen United Church. It has three windows on each side, and at the tops of the windows are squares of colored glass – yellow, blue, and red – that make pretty patterns when the sun shines through them. The upstairs is a regular church where people come for services, and sometimes other things. Downstairs, in the basement, is the Sequoia Outreach

School. It's a special school where kids who've dropped out of high school can get a second chance. Mrs. Buchanan believes in second chances. "You can't change your past, but you can change your future," she always says. Mostly what she means is that we all have to get an education and learn to look at things differently. She tells everyone they can do anything if they set their mind to it.

Sequoia Outreach School was located in the basement of the Gleichen United Church.

Sequoia school takes up the whole church basement, but it's only one classroom. The kitchen is at one end, and there's an area filled with playpens and baby carriers. There are boxes of toys and clothes that you can take home if you need them. There aren't any desks, except one for Mrs. B. and one for Lila. The students work together at long tables. There is also a folding screen that can be moved around when one of the girls has to nurse her baby, and a diaper-changing table in the bathroom that boys or girls can use.

Most of the First Nations kids go to school on the reserve, but I go to Central Bow Valley School, which is just down the road from Sequoia. My parents wanted my younger brothers and me to go to school off the reserve because they think it's important for us to learn about the non-native ways. They think that it will create better understanding between our peoples and that understanding each other will help us all get along. Sequoia is also for both First Nations and non-native kids.

A few days after Lila told me about the flower project, the little kids poked the seeds into the soil. The seeds looked really strange – like tiny curled-up brains. Then I was stuck spraying the dirt with water every day. I like making a fine mist with the spray bottle, but I won't tell anyone that. Every day, when I lift the clear plastic lids covered on the inside with droplets of water, the dirt looks the same as it did the day before. Growing flowers is even more boring than I imagined. I wish those little curled-up brains would hurry up and do some growing.

*Chapter 2*
# Lessons from Kahasi

I could feel the strength of the deer when I lifted the thick hide to my face. I breathed deeply and filled my nose with the smell of the smoke that was used to cure the hide. Kahasi (CAW-a-see) told me the smoke would make my moccasins strong and waterproof.

"Quit sniffing the hide. I need it to measure your foot," Kahasi said. She is an elder, one of the senior members of our community. She is a grandmother with nice wrinkles around her eyes and mouth. She is also *my* grandmother, my father's mother.

"But it smells so good. I like the smell better than flowers." Still, I did as I was told. I cleared a patch on the floor where I could lay the hide.

"You like the smell of the smoke? Don't worry. That will last a long time," she said, in her slow, soft voice.

Kahasi traced the shape of my foot on the hide so the moccasins would fit just right. She said it didn't matter that my foot would grow because the leather would stretch as my foot did. She said that by the time the moccasins were too small, they'd be worn out anyway. She used her sharpest scissors to cut out the soles of the moccasins. Kahasi was going to sew the pieces together, but first I was going to sew a pattern with beads to decorate the upper.

The blue tin that says "Danish Butter Cookies" on the lid and on the side is Kahasi's beading box, with sewing needles and small separate containers of shiny beads inside. I wanted to shake the containers and hold the beads, but I knew I must not until she said I could. She saw me looking at the beads, and knew I wanted to play with them like a little kid.

"You'll have to learn to bead on some cloth," she said. "I'll show you how to make a simple pattern first. Do you know what you would like to make?"

"I want to make a pink flower with white in the middle," I said. Of all the colors in the world, pink is the happiest color, and it's my favorite. "With green leaves, of course."

"That would be good for your moccasins, but first I'll show you how to make a simple diamond pattern. You can think about what colors to use and how you want it to look." Her scissors crunched through the deer hide, making the sound of walking on snow. "Did you know that sometimes, instead of beads, the Slavey women use moose hair to make pictures?" I remembered that the Slavey people live far to the north of us. "I am not sure how they do it," Kahasi continued, "but I have seen it some places. I think they dye the hairs different colors, then pick up a tuft with their fingers and stitch it sideways. Then they use small scissors to shape it. They make pictures of flowers mostly, and sometimes birds."

"I think I would rather use beads," I said. Though my grand-mother hadn't yet given me permission, I reached across the table and touched the tiny beads. They were red, blue, green, white, yellow, and clear. The beads were so small that the hole where the needle went was almost as big as the bead. "Will you show me today?" I asked.

"Yes, today I will show you, but you have to be more patient, ah?"

Kahasi always tells me to be more patient. I am very patient, but she doesn't think so. I like it when I do things and make other things happen, like spraying the dirt with water so seeds will grow into flowers, and chopping vegetables to make soup. She says this part is good – wanting to see things happen – but I shouldn't expect things to change quickly.

"We are an ancient people," she says. "Things change slowly. Besides, you don't live a long time if you are always hurrying up."

She finished cutting out the shape of each of my feet. One sole was a little bigger than the other. "They don't match," I said.

"Your feet don't match either. Nothing in nature is perfect. Nothing is exactly the same as anything else, not even your feet. Many times things look the same, but when you look carefully, you can find little differences," she said.

I looked at my feet closely. Except that my right foot has a mole near the ankle, they look exactly the same. But when I press my soles together, the big toe on my left foot stretches just a little bit higher than the one on my right foot. "I never noticed that before," I said. "My left foot *is* bigger."

"You see, there is a lot to learn by paying close attention to small things. Small things can make big differences." She laid her big scissors and the cut-out pieces in her basket, then turned to me. "OK. Now you can choose three colors. I guess, me, I should show you before you lose all the beads on the floor."

I didn't know I had spilled any, but when I looked closely, I saw little colored dots sprinkled on the floor. I got off my chair to search for them under the table, but my grandma said this was the time for learning, not for picking up. She took a plain piece of fabric from her basket. "What color first?" she asked.

"Red," I said – she didn't have any pink beads. She took a small container of red plastic beads from the cookie tin. I wanted to use glass beads on my moccasins because of how they sparkle in the sunlight, but she gave me plastic ones. It would have been impolite to ask for the glass ones, so I didn't say anything.

"Everyone starts beading on fabric first, and with plastic beads," Kahasi said, as if she could read my mind. She drew a long, straight line on the fabric with a marker, and then three more lines to make a diamond. "Bring your chair over, right beside me."

She gave me a long, thin needle with a thread. "I am going to show you the overlay stitch," she said. "It is the best way to bead. It is harder to learn, but it is the best way. Much stronger, and the beads lie flat, and they won't fall off easily."

She put two different kinds of needles on one piece of thread – one was the long, thin beading needle and the other was a regular sewing needle. Then she doubled the thread and pulled it through the back of the fabric. She slid three beads onto the skinny needle, then pushed it back through the cloth.

"You have to make it tight. If it's too loose, the beads or the thread can get caught in something and come off," she said. She poked the second needle close to the end of the string of three beads and made a quick, tight stitch at the end, then some tiny stitches between the beads. I was amazed that her bent-up hands could do such fine work. Next she pushed the needle up at the end to make another tight loop. "There, that is all there is to it. Simple, ah?"

Kahasi was sometimes as tricky as a magpie. Beading looks simple when she does it, but I knew it wouldn't be as simple for me. I tried to copy what she had done. I found it impossible to get the beads perfectly straight, but I practiced my patience without being told.

"Don't worry. It will get easier," she encouraged as she watched me struggle with the threads. "You want to know who is really good at beading?"

I pulled the thread through the fabric, held it tight with my left hand, and looked at her.

"Your father."

"My father! Dad? Dad can bead?"

Kahasi chuckled her low laugh. "Don't be so surprised. He's really good at beading, ever since he learned when he was about your age. He made many perfect designs. Very smooth. Good enough to sell. He doesn't do this now that he is a grown man. It is too bad."

"Dad?" I repeated. I tried to picture it in my mind, but every time I did, I laughed. I couldn't imagine him sitting still with tiny beads and sewing needles in his big hands.

"He can sew, too," she said. "He's pretty good at that, but he's better at beading."

"My dad can sew *and* bead? You must be kidding me." I searched her face for clues that she was joking, but her eyes weren't sparkling wickedly, and her mouth wasn't twitching into a smile.

"No, I am not kidding. You can ask him sometime. He will tell you."

"How about my mum? Can she bead, too?"

Kahasi laughed. "Your mum can do many things, but beading is not one of them. I don't think she could even thread a needle. At least, I have never seen her do these things."

As I worked the simple pattern, I tried to imagine Dad as a boy, working at the table with his mother. Maybe the two of

Making the beads lie flat – with no lumps or bumps – is part of the art of beading.

them had sat together and beaded and eaten all the Danish butter cookies that had once been in the blue tin.

I suppose I shouldn't have been so surprised about Dad being
able to sew. He is happiest when he is making things – country
and western music mostly, but he likes to perform traditional
dances too, and make paintings. He is happy to be able to earn
money making music, but he is sad, too. He is usually away on
the weekends, singing and playing his guitar, so he spends less
time with us. At least he had his brother with him, my Uncle
Douglas. The two of them and my two older brothers, Liland
and Jack, have a band called Red Lightning.

Usually people have music bands when they are young, but
not my dad. He waited until he was grown up and had eight
children before he started his band. "No one would play with
me, so I had to have enough kids to get a band that liked my
singing," he tells strangers. But he is really a great singer. He
should be on the radio.

Mum's most important job is loving us, and she does that
the best of anything. She stays home with us most of the time,
but lately she has been feeling sick and has to lie down on her
bed or on the sofa. The doctor at the clinic says she'll probably
have to have an operation one of these days, but Mum doesn't
like the idea of going to the hospital in Calgary no matter what
he says. When Mum isn't feeling well and Dad is away, that

leaves Angel and me to do the cooking and to look after our four little brothers. And now that Angel is busy with her own baby, I usually have to do everything. I love it when I can escape and come to Kahasi's house.

"Small, tight stitches," my grandmother reminded me. "The smaller and neater, the better. I don't want to see any stitches on top when you are done. And no lumps and bumps. When you run your hand over the top, it should feel smooth, almost like a piece of glass." I concentrate on getting the beads right. I want to make her proud of me. I want her to say I am as good at beading as my dad.

Beading is tricky, but at least it is very quiet at Kahasi's house, and a person doesn't get mad because of all the noise. Kahasi has been staying alone since my grandfather passed on because her children have houses of their own. Soon she will go to stay with one of her children, or they might come to share her house.

Our house is the same as Kahasi's, the same as almost everyone else's on the reserve. It has six rooms – a kitchen, a living room, three bedrooms, and a bathroom. My parents have one bedroom. My four little brothers have the biggest bedroom, with two sets of bunk beds, so that each of them has his own bed. My two older brothers stay in the basement, where the washing machine is.

My sister and I have the smallest bedroom, but it's the best one. The walls are pink with white clouds, and there's a big unicorn that Dad painted on one wall when we were little. Angel and I still like to look at the unicorn, so we haven't painted over it. Her baby, Kayden, shares the room with us, and she likes the pink and the unicorn too.

Sometimes it gets very noisy at our house, especially if the TV is on, which it always is. The little kids like to watch cartoons, Mum likes to watch soap operas, and my older brothers and my dad like to watch sports. My little brothers laugh at the TV, and my dad yells at it: "Come on! Get it! Run, run!" Sometimes he even jumps in the air, as if that will help his team score.

The worst time is when wrestling is on. All the boys and men like to watch it, and they all have their favorite wrestler. They yell and cheer lots during the show, and afterwards the boys roll around on the floor, practicing their moves. My father likes to play this way, too. They all think they are wrestling stars. It's crazy, and I can't think with all that noise. I hate wrestling night.

At Kahasi's house, the sounds are different. Usually she doesn't watch TV or listen to the radio. "It's just bad news," she says, "and it makes me feel sad. If it's something I need to know, someone will tell me."

At her house there is just the clock ticking quietly, the kettle coming to a boil, and her soft voice patiently telling me things.

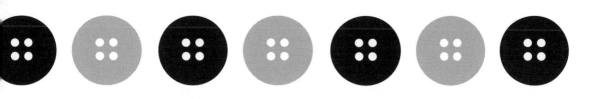

## Chapter 3

# Kelvin the Bully

My little brothers – Joseph, Colton, Raine, and Davis – were watching cartoons and pretending to be superheroes in the living room while I tried to write a poem for school. It was useless – I need quiet time to write poetry.

I went to the kitchen to start supper. Mum and Dad were next door. Mum was visiting with Auntie Michelle, and Dad and his brother, Uncle Douglas, were planning a road trip for their band, Red Lightning. The night before, they'd had a big map spread on the table, and they talked about traveling all over southern Alberta in my uncle's old green van. They were excited about their new idea to drum up some business, instead of just waiting for people to call them. I was kind of mad about the idea. When

Dad and my oldest brothers are away, it means more work for me, and they were talking about being gone for two weeks. Red Lightning had been gone for two or three days before, but never for two weeks. That would be far too long.

When I got to the kitchen, Kelvin was sitting at our kitchen table, holding Kayden on his lap and giving her sips from his can of pop.

"You shouldn't give her that. It's not healthy," I told him.

"Ha ha. She loves this," he said, grinning and shifting the hair from his eyes. "Look how she messes up her face and then wants more." I just shook my head and gave up. I knew he wouldn't listen to me.

I was running water into a pot when Angel came in. "Kelvin! What are you doing? You can't give her pop! She's a baby."

"Why not? She loves it. Watch." He held the can to the baby's lips and tipped it slightly. Kayden squinted her eyes, grimaced, then licked her lips.

"That's horrible – it's bad for her," said Angel, reaching for Kayden. "I want her to grow up healthy. Pop will rot her teeth."

"Ha! She's only got two teeth. A lot you know." He gave the baby another sip.

"Stop it!" cried Angel. "Stop! Now!" She tried to reach for Kayden, but Kelvin held the baby tightly against his body.

"I'll give her pop if I want to. I'm the man! I get to decide things. You listen to me!" Kelvin yelled. "That's how it goes. Remember that in your thick head. Whatever I want to give her is good for her, and that's that!"

Kayden doesn't like loud voices. She started whimpering, then bawling.

"Here, you take her. I hate it when she yells like that." Kelvin pushed the baby into Angel's arms, lifted the pop can to his lips, and drained it. He threw the can across the room and into the sink. On his way out of the kitchen, he grabbed Angel's chin. The anger was in his eyes. "You remember that I'm the boss," he snarled.

I put the pot on the stove and glared at Kelvin, waiting to see what would happen next. I didn't know what I could do, but I was ready to try anything to help Angel. Kelvin was using his loud voice that meant he wanted to fight. The raised voices brought my little brothers running to the kitchen, and they looked ready to fight, too. Five-year-old Colton was carrying a sword made of wood and black tape, waving it over his head as if he meant to hit Kelvin with it.

"You remember that, too," Kelvin said, staring and jabbing his finger at me. "I'm the *boss*!" I was glad to hear the door slam behind him.

Angel had tears in her eyes. "You want us to go fight him?" offered Colton, brandishing his sword.

"Hii-yah!" Seven-year-old Raine kicked his foot high in the air. Little Davis tried a kick too, and fell on his behind.

"We can do it! We can beat him. We can make him sorry," said Joseph, who was nine.

Angel sniffled and shook her head. She gave our brothers a small crooked smile.

"Maybe you should all go outside and play," I suggested. "You can make sure there aren't any wild dogs ready to attack, or any mountain lions. You can keep us safe that way."

"Yah!" said Colton. "Come on, Raine. Let's save our family from wild animals."

"I'm the oldest, so I get to be the mountain lion and chase you. Grrrr," cried Joseph, running out the door growling.

Angel sat in the chair where Kelvin had been. I turned back to the stove, added salt to the water, and turned on the burner. "Want to talk?" I asked.

Angel shook her head, but then she said, "I don't know what to do."

"He'll cool off. Eventually." Too bad, though. I wished he'd keep stomping. I wished his anger would take him so far away that he couldn't get back.

"It's not that," she said. She toyed with some crumbs on the table, using her fingers to brush them into a little pile. "He wants me to move in with his mum and sisters. He says there's more room there, and we can be together all the time."

"But you can't do that," I said. I felt panicky at the thought of her going to stay with Kelvin forever.

She looked at me with sad eyes. "But I'm nearly eighteen, and I have his baby. We're a family, kind of. He says he loves me, and he wants us to live like a real family, and there's no room for him here." She spread the crumbs back across the table, then started gathering them up again. "I'd like us to be a family, too. I don't want to stay with his family, but I don't think I have a choice. There is nowhere else for us to go."

"But Angel, we are your family too, and we love you and Kayden. Besides, Mum needs you."

"I wouldn't be very far away. I could still come over and help."

"But what about school? What about college? What about becoming a nurse so you can really help people?"

"Kelvin says to forget about college. He says I'm not smart enough to get in, and even if I was smart enough to finish high school and got good enough grades, I'd never survive in the city. He says people there will pick on me because I'm First Nations, and they'll treat me badly, no matter what I do. He says if I try living in the white world, I'll be destroyed, the way his father was. Sometimes I think he's right. I don't want to go to the city, especially by myself."

Steam was rising from the boiling water and clattering the lid. I jumped up to grab it, then sat at the table again with my sister.

"Look at me, Angel, and promise. Promise me you won't do anything yet."

"I don't think I can promise." Her head was down, and her voice was choked. "Kelvin keeps pressuring me, and he's stronger than me, you know?"

"You're wrong. You're stronger, Angel. You're smarter, too."

"You would say that." She smiled her sad, crooked smile, but tears were streaming down her face. "You're my best sister and my best friend."

"But it's true. Look at how well you do in school when you have time to study. You're a lot smarter than Kelvin, and you're loving, too. Kahasi says there's a lot of strength in loving. It's stronger than steel."

I reached out to take her hand. Kayden slapped her tiny hand on top as if we were players on a team, getting ready to win. I hoped that Angel could win. And that I could help her. But how? How could I convince Angel that she is not powerless – that none of us is?

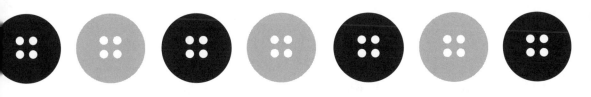

*Chapter 4*

# Grannies and Babies

The wind blew snow across the prairie like a cloud lifting from the ground. It flung arrows of ice that pierced my eardrums as I walked from my school to Sequoia, and made my long hair dance and twist into knots that would hurt to take out. As soon as I came inside, my glasses fogged up and made me blind. My fingers and nose were so frozen that they burned as if they were on fire. I was cold and tired, and just wanted to curl up and sleep like the babies dozing on the mats and in the playpens.

The weather seemed to be a little mixed up. It was supposed to be getting warmer, not colder. I wished the snow would melt, and the prairie grasses would begin to grow. But instead, we had more snow, and winds as fierce as a hungry bear. It was a good thing my little seeds were warm and safe inside.

"Lacey, guess what?" Angel asked me. Her brown eyes were sparkling with happiness, and she looked as if she wanted to jump around. She took my cold hands in her warm ones. "Brrrr! Did you forget to use your pockets?"

"I'm OK. What did you want to tell me?"

"My math test! I passed! I passed math. Isn't that the greatest news? And I not only passed, I got 82 percent!"

"I'm so proud of you, my smart sister. I knew you could do it!" I gave her a high-five.

"I'm proud of me too. When Mrs. B. gave me back the test, I gave her a hug and a big kiss. I think *that* surprised her."

"How about Kelvin?" I asked. I looked around the room, but he wasn't there. "Did he pass?"

Her face lost its glow. "No," she said. "He didn't make it. I think he's mad at me because I passed and he didn't. But I studied and worked hard. He should have done that too, instead of watching TV and going to parties."

After I watered the dirt in the little containers, I wrapped a blanket around my shoulders, sat with the babies, and stayed quiet. I've learned that it's often best to be quiet, especially if I don't want to go outside. When I'm quiet, sometimes I'm also invisible, and no one gives extra work to people they can't see.

I had enough work already with my dad and my older brothers gone away to sing. Mum wasn't feeling well enough to do everything herself, so for Angel and me it meant lots of cooking, cleaning, laundry, and looking after noisy little brothers. I was starting to think Mum should go have that operation.

Kayden stood in a play saucer on the floor beside Angel. I crept across the floor to her and tried to make her laugh by playing peek-a-boo and batting the toys attached to the play saucer. I like it when she laughs. She makes a happy sound deep in her throat that turns into a high-pitched squeal, and she flaps her arms and tries to jump up and down. Even her hair laughs. It's just like Angel's hair, and swings in little curls that bounce like a spring. Watching her laugh always makes me laugh, too, but I am careful to laugh quietly, without opening my mouth. If I have a big laugh, I have to make sure to cover my mouth to keep the sound inside and to hide my crooked teeth.

There was music coming from a CD – the sound of drums and the voices of men singing ancient songs. Kayden bounced to the beat of the drums. The music made me think of sitting around a fire, and it made me feel warmer. Two of the little kids were making long blue snakes out of the play clay that Lila had mixed. Some of the older kids were drawing, working on the computers, reading, and writing things in their binders. Everyone was quietly busy inside because no one wanted to go outside. The babies didn't know enough to be quiet, so some were crying or babbling. A few were banging on toys. I picked up one of the babies who was crying and jiggled him up and down as I walked around the room.

My sister was using the side of her pencil to add shading to a picture she'd drawn of an old woman sewing. The shading made the woman look real.

"That's beautiful, Angel," I heard Mrs. Buchanan say. "She looks so loving and kind, and you've got her eyes just right. You can see her wisdom in her eyes." Angel didn't say anything; she just kept drawing. I wondered if she was still mad at Kelvin for not making her a Valentine's Day gift yesterday. She pretended it didn't bother her, but I knew it did.

"Your portrait reminds me of the women in some photos I saw when I was in Calgary last week," Mrs. B continued, as she watched Angel sketch. "I heard about a remarkable program that involves grandmothers in Canada helping grandmothers in Africa by sewing purses."

"How could purses help them?" asked Angel.

"The Canadian grandmothers sell the purses here and send the money to the African grandmothers to help them raise their grandchildren. Millions and millions of people in Africa – especially in southern Africa are infected with HIV. You know, that disease connected with AIDS? Many young adults – some who are mothers and fathers with small children – are dying."

"Why don't they just go to the clinic and take medicine?" asked Trisha, who was working at the same table as Angel. Trisha wore glasses like me, but she had short hair and a belly shaped like a big watermelon. Her baby hadn't been born yet.

"That's part of the problem. So far, the medicines for controlling HIV and AIDS are still very expensive and only easy to get in rich countries like Canada. They are very difficult to get in Africa," said Mrs. B. "Maybe two out of a hundred Africans with these diseases get the medicines they need."

"But what does that have to do with the grandmothers?" Angel asked.

"In some ways, Africa is like Siksika," explained Mrs. B. "Families are close, and often large. Many communities are isolated, and it's difficult to get from place to place. At Siksika, when something happens to parents, the rest of the family steps in to help – often the aunties and uncles, who have children of their own, take in the orphaned children. But in Africa the aunties and uncles may be ill or dying, too. They can't look after anyone else's children. Maybe they can't even look after their own. So, who is going to take care of all these kids? The grandmothers – because there isn't anyone else to do it. What makes it even harder is that some of the children are also infected with HIV."

"I don't get it," said Trisha. She was leaning back in her chair now, stroking her round, pregnant tummy as if it were a kitten. "How can little kids get infected?"

"They get the disease from their mothers, sometimes while they are being born and sometimes from breast milk."

"You're kidding!" said Trisha. "If I had HIV, I'd do something before the baby was born. Get tested or something."

"Would you? What if there was no clinic? Or what if you could be tested, but there was no medicine? Would you choose not to feed your baby, just in case it got sick? Would you let your baby die of starvation, just in case it caught the disease?"

"I'd think of something."

"Like what?" Mrs. B. challenged.

"I'd move to Canada," Trisha announced triumphantly, and everyone laughed.

Mrs. B. smiled. "Anyway, that's where the Canadian grand-mothers come in. They make purses and sell them, and send the money to the African grandmothers, who spend it on food, housing, school fees – whatever is needed. In this simple way, ordinary grandmothers here are helping to save lives there. But what's just as important is that they are giving hope to the African grandmothers, and to the children."

"We have a lot of grandmothers. Maybe they should do some-thing like that," said Angel.

"Maybe so," said Mrs. B. "Maybe so." She left the little group and walked slowly around the classroom, talking quietly with students and checking whether they needed help.

I thought about what I'd heard. I liked the sound of people helping other people. That's the way the Sequoia Outreach School works. Sometimes the elders need help cleaning or shoveling snow, and the students help. Sometimes the people in town grow too much in their gardens, so they bring the extra food to the school for everyone to share. We make salads and maybe some cookies or cakes that we can share with them. It's a circle of everyone helping everyone. I like that kind of circle.

Kayden patted me with her little hand, wanting attention. I made a circle with my mouth and made the "oooo" sound of an owl, and she waved her arms and legs so hard that I thought she would tip the play saucer over. I grabbed the side of it to keep it upright.

I thought of how it would be if my sister or my mother passed on because of a bad disease like AIDS. How would it feel to lose people that you love? It hurt a lot when my grandfather died, but at least he had time to live a good long life. It would be even worse to die young. Everything would die with them – their dreams, their hopes, and their futures. And those poor little kids left alone, except for their grandparents. It was the saddest story I'd ever heard.

I remembered Kahasi telling me that I shouldn't be so shy, that sometimes women needed to speak up. That was what the grandmothers were doing. By using their sewing, the grandmothers here were speaking up to help the faraway grandmothers. I wanted to speak up, too, but I wanted to speak up quietly, so no one would notice. I kept making silly faces for Kayden, but I kept my eye on Mrs. B. When she sat down at her desk, I decided to speak up. I lifted Kayden into my arms – holding someone smaller made me feel stronger, braver. I stood beside Mrs. B.'s desk and waited until her funny halfway glasses looked up at me.

"I can sew, and I am learning how to bead. Do you think I'd be allowed to help in Africa?" I asked.

"Help? Help the grandmothers, you mean?"

I nodded my head and tried to move Kayden to my hip. She was so big now that her feet reached down to my knees. "Maybe if I could sew some purses, I could help a little."

"Hmmm," said Mrs. Buchanan. She rested her chin on her hand and looked up at the ceiling. Then she said, "Well, you are not a grandmother, but I expect they need all the help they can get to raise those babies. Why don't you send them a letter and ask?"

I had learned how to write a letter in grade 4, but I didn't learn how to write a letter to grandmothers in Africa. Mrs. B.

said just to write what was in my heart. I thought about it for a few days, especially when I was sewing with Kahasi. I decided it would be easier to write to the grandmothers in Canada. Their headquarters were in Toronto. This is what I wrote:

Dear Grandmothers Helping Grandmothers in Africa,

My name is Lacey Little Bird. I am a grade 7 student at Central Bow Valley School in Gleichen, Alberta, Canada. My sister is a grade 11 student at Sequoia Outreach School because she has a nine-month-old daughter named Kayden.

Last fall, I helped my grandmother make a jingle dress, and I am learning to do beading. I like to sew, and my grandmother says I am good at traditional art. I'm a member of the Siksika Nation – Blackfoot tribe of Southern Alberta.

The principal at my sister's school told us about the "Grandmothers to Grandmothers" program, and I thought that we could make some purses, too. We could invite our grandmothers to help us decorate them. This way, we would form our own Grandmothers to Grandmothers group.

Would it be OK for us to do this?

On our reserve, grandmothers are so important.

Lots of our young parents suffer because of the effects of poverty, drugs, and alcohol. Even though our lives are sometimes hard, I think they're not as difficult as the lives of those grandmothers in Africa.

Please tell me if it would be OK to help.

Yours truly,
Lacey Little Bird

I showed the letter to Mrs. B. She said that it was a fine letter but that I needed to include my mailing address, or an e-mail address, so they could write back to me. We don't have a car, and it's hard for my parents to get to the post office to pick up mail. We don't have a computer either, so I wrote the address for Sequoia at the top. Mrs. B. got the Toronto address from the grandmothers in Calgary, gave me an envelope and a stamp, and promised to mail the letter for me.

As I licked the gluey flap of the envelope and closed it, I thought about how far my words would travel – all the way to Ontario and that big city of Toronto. I hoped the grandmothers would like my letter, and I hoped they would let me help. I knew Kahasi would be proud of me. And she would teach me what I needed to know; she could sew anything. Maybe my mum could help, too, because she was a grandmother of Kayden. I bet she would like to help the African grandmothers – if she felt well enough – even though she liked sewing about as much as Angel did, which was not at all. If the Canadian grandmothers said yes, maybe even Angel would finally get interested in sewing.

I gave the envelope a little kiss before handing it to Mrs. B.

Every day I bugged Lila about the mail. "Is there a letter from those grandmothers yet?" I asked as soon as I got to Sequoia, and every day Lila said, "No, not today. I'll let you know as soon as it arrives. Really. I promise. You will be the first to know."

It seemed to be taking an awfully long time. Waiting for a letter was as painful as waiting for seeds to turn into plants. I thought it would be nice if the grandmothers could give me an answer right away. If they said yes, I could get started on the sewing. The sooner I started, the more purses I could make, and the more purses I made, the more money the African grandmothers would get for food and shelter and other things for their grandchildren. What could be taking them so long? I decided I didn't like to wait for letters; an e-mail would have been better. Maybe I should have asked to use the computer at school.

I sprayed water on the dirt where the seeds were buried every day for six school days before the miracle happened. It was Tuesday afternoon, just after a holiday long weekend, and I couldn't believe my eyes when I lifted the wet lid from the seed tray. It wasn't just black dirt anymore. During the weekend, specks of green had pushed up through the dirt in some of the compartments. They looked like bright green butterflies on short stems. The soil and the baby plants smelled like springtime after it rains.

"Mrs. B.! Mrs. B., look!" I called across the noisy classroom. "The seeds are alive. The flowers are growing."

Mrs. Buchanan smiled. "Lacey, shush," she said, putting one finger to her lips. "Not so loud." She hoisted Kayden onto one hip and wove her way through the tables covered with books, water bottles, and baby carriers. "I'll be there in just a minute."

She stopped to talk to Kelvin on the way. He had a lot of papers and books spread on the table, and a pen in his hand, but his head was lying on top of the papers. It was hard to tell if he was tired or mad or needed help. Mrs. B. sat beside Kelvin and held Kayden on her lap as she pointed to things in his book and asked him questions. When she left, he was sitting up and writing again.

I wasn't smiling what Mrs. B. calls my "shy smile" when she came over. I had the big smile that lets my crooked teeth show. She bent her head to smell the dirt, too. "Excellent. Excellent!" she said. "That's the soil giving birth to new life. Amazing, isn't it?"

I nodded. "Will they really grow into flowers?"

"You just wait and see."

"How long will it take?"

"It will take as long as it needs to take. You just keep watering them every day, and let them surprise you. Oh, this baby smells bad," she added, wrinkling her nose. "Kelvin, your daughter needs a new diaper." She handed Kayden to Kelvin and went back to her desk.

Every time I went to Sequoia to help look after the babies, I looked after the little plants, too. They are called nasturtiums. Mrs. B. told me that they would have flowers the colors of the sun – red, yellow, and orange. She also said that we could eat the plants – the flowers and leaves would taste good in a salad – but if we left the flowers, they would make more seeds for next year. She said some people even ate the seeds, and they tasted spicy.

When the plants got bigger and stronger, we would move them into bigger containers, and after Easter, when it was warm outside, we would put them on the street so everyone could see them. I just hoped people wouldn't realize that my flowers were good to eat.

*Chapter 5*

# "I Was Going to Need a Lot of Help"

"Let me see what you have there. Your beading is looking good, very neat," Kahasi said when I went to her house after supper one night. She pulled at the beads I had sewn in the diamond pattern, trying to pry them loose with her fingernails. None of the beads came loose.

"Do you think it's time to start working on the hide?" she asked.

I couldn't believe what my ears were hearing. It was time to do some real beading.

"First we need to make a paste. Some people draw the design on the hide with a pen, but I like to do things the old way. Sometimes, the old ways are better," she said. "We must remember the old ways."

Kahasi lifted a little bowl from the shelf and scooped a spoonful of flour from the bag. Then she poured in a small stream of water. "Now, you stir it until it is smooth," she said.

She dipped a toothpick into the paste, then moved her glasses up and down so she could look through the bottom part and see better. She used the toothpick to draw a flower on the upper piece that she had cut from the hide. She kept dipping the toothpick into the white paste to make a smooth line. She drew each petal slowly and carefully, and then she added leaves. "There," she said, "now we have your design ready to bead."

I picked up the piece of deer hide. The flower was perfectly shaped, each petal looked exactly the same shape and size. "You can get started beading if you want. I'll get the other one ready."

"Can I use the glass beads now?" I asked.

"Go ahead, my girl." She nodded as she drew the other flower. "But be careful doing the curved edge. Go slowly. Even though you know what you are doing now, you will find it harder."

It was tougher to push the needle through hide than through fabric. I started with the outline of the flower, using three beads at a time. I tried to sew exactly on the curved line that Kahasi had made, but it was harder to make a curved line than the straight lines of the diamond pattern. I could tell it was going to take me a long time to bead just one moccasin.

"Ouch," I said as the needle stuck my finger. A tiny drop of blood formed on the tip of my finger, like a small red bead. I wiped the blood on my jeans. "I think I should have asked you to do the beading. By the time I finish just one petal, the moccasins may be too small."

Kahasi laughed softly. "Beading will teach you about patience,

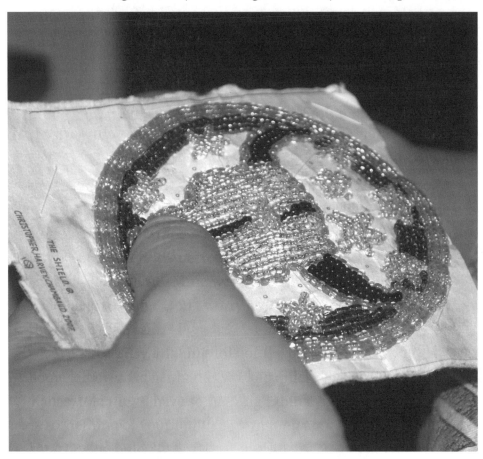

Any pattern can be beaded, but First Nations
people most often use designs from nature.

Lacey. There will be many times when you have to take off some of the beads you have sewn because they aren't right. Making something sometimes means going backwards, starting over."

"Not me. I like to go forward. I like to make new things without wasting any time."

She didn't say anything. She just smiled and looked down at her sewing.

"Kahasi, do you think you could teach me how to make purses?"

"Making purses from hide would be a waste of valuable material. People need moccasins and other clothing, not purses. Where did you get such an idea, ah?"

"I don't mean hide purses. I mean cloth purses, something that would be fast," I explained.

She smiled again. "To be fast, you need a machine. A sewing machine. The only sewing machine I have is my hands, and they are not fast anymore." She made some more stitches on the tiny quilt she was making for my cousin's new baby. "Why do you want to make fast purses, anyway?"

I told her about grandmothers helping grandmothers and about the letter I had sent. "That sounds like a good idea," she said. "We all have to help each other. You know how to embroider and now how to bead. I could help you, too. But the fast sewing you will have to learn from someone else."

There were small pieces of fabric on the table where she had been cutting different shapes, and I knew she had more scraps of heavy cotton like the one she had given me to learn beading.

"Kahasi, are you going to use those old pieces for anything?" I asked.

"Yes, some day. I save everything in my basket, and some day it gets used."

I was hoping she would say she was going to throw the bits away. I was going to ask her if I could have them. Instead I asked, "Would you mind...would it be okay if I looked at the things in your basket?"

"Yes, yes, go ahead. There are pieces there of just about every-thing I have made going back a long time. Each of those pieces has a little story."

I pulled out scraps of hide, ends of cotton printed with designs, and heavy canvas-type material. I played with the pieces on the table, making patterns with them. They looked a bit like an old-time quilt. They also made me think of a colorful cloth bag one of my teachers used to carry papers and things.

"I don't know anyone who has a sewing machine, do you?" I asked.

"I can't think of anyone right now."

"And where would I get the materials?"

"I don't know that, either." Kahasi kept sewing and humming. "If it is meant to be, there will be a way for these things to happen. Don't worry so much, my girl, or you will become an old woman before you have the chance to become a young one."

If it is meant to be, I am going to need a lot of help from someone. There aren't any stores at Siksika or Gleichen that sell the things I need to make purses. The nearest stores like that are in Strathmore. It would take thirty minutes to drive there if I had a car, but I don't have a car, and I don't have anyone to drive me. And, I don't have any money. Why didn't I think of all these things before I sent the letter to the grandmothers asking if I could help the Africans? Maybe it was a good thing they hadn't answered me.

# Angel in Despair

Angel was on the floor of the kitchen, cutting her old jeans into little pieces. The television was playing in the living room, and crazy music was coming from the basement. It sounded as if the boys were drumming on pipes, the walls, the floor, the washing machine, anything they could find. "What are you doing?" I asked her.

"I don't know. I'm just making something," she said over the racket.

"But what are you making? A blanket?"

"I don't know," she repeated. "OK, I do know, but I don't know if it will work out." I waited for her to tell me. "I'm trying to make a purse. I thought maybe I could help you make some purses to sell, you know, so the money could go to the African grandmothers. I thought I could learn by making a bag for carrying Kayden's stuff." She pricked her finger with a pin. "Oww! I hate sewing!" she wailed. "It's hopeless! I understand how, but I can't seem to do it right."

"I've helped Kahasi sew some things. If you tell me what to do, maybe I can help. Maybe we can work on it together."

"No! I don't want your help! Don't you get it, Lacey? I want to do this on my own, by myself, without anyone telling me what to do or how to do it!" She stood up, threw the material on the floor, and stomped out of the room. She must have been spending too much time with the little kids; she was starting to act like them. I picked up the denim pieces and spread them on the floor like pieces of a puzzle. I could imagine how they would look as a shoulder bag.

I threaded a needle with thick black thread and used the running stitch Kahasi had shown me to put the pieces together when we'd made the jingle dress a few months before. It is a wonderful dress, all covered with metal cones that make tinkling music when I move. But this sewing was different because I would have to put the scraps together to make a bigger piece. As I added a third piece and a fourth piece, I could see the shape that Angel had designed. But by the time I finished one side, my fingers were sore from holding the needle tight and pushing it through the heavy fabric. I left the sewing on the kitchen table. When my sister found it, it would be like the fairytale about the elves and the shoemaker, the one where all the shoemaker's work is done by elves during the night.

I was just finishing the sewing when Mum came up from the basement carrying a laundry basket overflowing with clothes. She was holding onto the railing and moving as slowly as Kahasi. My little brothers peeled up behind her and ran into the living room.

"Want me to take that?" I asked, reaching for the jumble of clothes.

"No, I can do this," she said. I followed her to her bedroom where she dumped the clothes on the bed.

"Are you feeling better?" I asked as I helped fold the clothes and sort them into piles.

"Maybe a little." She smiled, but her voice sounded tired. "I have to do some things. I can't just lie around and do nothing all the time."

Folding laundry was something Angel and I usually did together. I wondered if this would be a good time to tell Mum about Angel and Kelvin, and how he wanted Angel to stay with his family. But Mum looked like she had used all of her energy doing laundry. I decided it wouldn't be a good time. Dad was going to be home in two days anyway. Maybe I'd just wait and tell him.

When we were done folding and folding, Mum went to lie on the sofa, and I carried the clothes for Angel, Kayden, and me to our room. Kayden was asleep already in her crib. She makes little puffing sounds when she sleeps, and funny faces because of her dreams. Angel had her sketchbook on her lap and a scowl on her face. I could tell by the strong, swift movements she was making with her hands that she was still mad about the sewing. She has even less patience than me.

She looked so prickly that I didn't say anything. I pulled my backpack onto the bed with me, took out my social studies book, and began the two pages of homework I had to do for Mrs. Martinez. I could still hear the TV down the hall. A hockey game was on, and a player had just scored. There was lots of hooting from my little brothers, who were watching the game with Mum because Dad wasn't home. The boys were clapping and jumping around. I could hear the horns blowing on the TV, and the announcer talking about the replay.

I glanced at Angel once in a while, waiting for her anger to pass and for her face to soften. "It sounds like someone scored," I said.

"No kidding," she said. She was still mad. She stared at me as if she wanted to make me melt, and I didn't like the feeling.

"What are you drawing?" I asked.

"Nothing. Just garbage." She threw her sketches on the floor and they scattered everywhere. Some landed beside my bed. It looked as if she had been drawing all sorts of purses and bags.

"Don't you have any homework?" I asked.

"I'm not doing homework anymore. I'm a woman. I don't need school."

"But what about graduating? What about being a nurse?"

"I don't care about those things. I'll just be a mother, like everyone else around here."

"But Mrs. B. says the only way to make things better is with an education. Nothing will change if we don't make it change."

"Nothing will ever change here, anyway," she said. "Boys will get in trouble with the police; girls will get pregnant, drop out of school, and stay home. It's the way things have always been, and it's the way they always will be. Why should I be any different?"

I couldn't think of a reason. What could a little sister tell a big sister about "why"? Just then, Angel's baby rolled over in her sleep.

"For Kayden," I said, quickly. "You have to do it for Kayden. You have to teach her that she has choices. Set an example." Angel didn't say anything. She just sat on the bed, staring and looking glum.

I closed my book and slid close beside Angel on her bed. She would either let me, or push me off. She didn't push me. "What's wrong? What happened?" I asked.

"Nothing. Nothing happened. Nothing ever happens around here, remember?"

I used Kahasi's trick of getting people to talk. I just sat beside her and didn't say anything. The trick worked.

"It's all too hard, Lacey," she said. "The schoolwork is hard. Looking after Kayden is hard. Staying here is hard. I don't think I can do it. I'm never going to become a nurse and help people. Kelvin is right. No matter what, I'll end up just like everybody else."

I reached for her hand and held it. I didn't know what to say, so I just waited for her to talk if she wanted to. Though she didn't say it, I think it made her feel better to let me hold her hand. Pretty soon she lay her beautiful black curls on my shoulder. "I just...I just don't know..."

I put my arms around my big sister and held her the way our mother used to hold us when we were small. I didn't like the way Angel's thoughts were going. I wished Mum was feeling better. I wished I could talk to her, or that Angel would.

Why was Dad always away when bad things happened? Two days, I reminded myself. Dad would be home in two days. I could talk to Dad. I'd tell him everything.

## Chapter 7

# Dad's News

I dashed down the hall from my bedroom to answer the phone. It had rung five times already, and no one had answered.

"Hey, Princess. Is Mum around?" It was Dad's voice on the telephone. There was a lot of noise in the background – the sound of dishes rattling and people talking. Maybe he was in a restaurant. But he sounded happy, probably because he'd be coming home tomorrow.

"She's resting, I think. Do you want me to wake her up?"

"No, no. That's fine."

"Dad, I can't wait for you to get home. There's so much happening. There is so much I need to tell you."

"Well...that's why I'm phoning, Princess. They've asked us to stay on. I won't be home tomorrow like I planned. This is such great news for Red Lightning. Can you tell Mum?"

"You're not coming home?" I said.

"Well, not right now..."

"But Dad, we need you here."

"Honey, we have to work when there's work. You know that. This is a big chance for the band. We'll get home as soon as we can."

"How long?" I asked, even though I wasn't sure I wanted the answer.

"I don't know. A week maybe? Ten days?"

"But Dad, I need to talk to you..."

"Don't worry. We'll have lots of time to talk when I get home. Hey, I've got to run now. Tell Mum, OK? Love you. Give hugs and kisses to everyone, OK?"

"Sure. I love you, too, Dad." I felt as if I were a balloon and all my air had been sucked out. This was awful news. How could I keep doing all of the things I was doing, and how could I keep Angel from moving in with Kelvin's family? More than anything, I needed Dad to come home. I needed him home now.

## Chapter 8

# White Buffalo Calf Woman

"How was it at school today?" Kahasi asked, even before I had put my jacket on the hook. Her voice came from the kitchen. She was on her hands and knees on the floor, washing it.

"It was boring."

"How could it be boring to learn new things?" She rinsed the rag in the bucket and kept moving it back and forth across the floor.

"I didn't learn any new things. It was just boring, boring, boring. There was something funny, though. The teacher was trying to teach us about the Blackfoot Confederacy, and she's white, I mean – " I searched my memory for the Blackfoot word. "She's *napikwan*. She talked about Treaty 7 and how Chief

Crowfoot signed the peace treaty in 1877, but I don't think she knew that it was signed right here. I don't think she knows that Chief Crowfoot's grave is up on the hill, or even that Blackfoot Crossing is part of Siksika."

"Why didn't you ask her if she knows?" Kahasi said, as she stood up slowly and put her hands on her lower back and stretched.

"Because everybody knows that...except maybe her. Besides, I didn't want to sound stupid, especially in front of all the white kids."

"Sometimes, my girl, it is only stupid *not* to ask the questions. It is important to speak up. Sometimes this is something you must do."

"But no one else spoke up. All the kids from the reserve just slid down in their seats, bent their heads, and acted like statues, so I did too."

"But you, you are not everyone. You could have taught her something, maybe. Did you ever think about that, ah?"

"No, I never thought about teaching my *teacher*."

"We all have things to teach each other," she said. I took the bucket to the bathroom and dumped the dirty water in the toilet. "Now, come in here and talk to me. I need to have a little rest," she called from the living room. She was sitting in her favorite chair, the one with the pattern of flowers, when I came into the room.

"Have you heard anything from those grandmothers, Lacey?" she asked.

"No," I said. "I guess the Canadian grandmothers are too busy sewing, and the African grandmothers are too busy looking after all those grandchildren. I'm not sure it was a good idea, anyway."

"Yes, you are probably right. You have enough things to do here. You can't be helping poor old grandmothers in Africa, or ones in Canada who don't even know how to write letters. I don't know what you were thinking." I wasn't sure if she was being serious or if she was telling me I was giving up too easily. Her face didn't show me any clues.

"What do you mean?"

"Maybe you are using your head to think. Heads think too much. They get things mixed up." I could hear the clock ticking in the background, as slow and steady as a heartbeat. "Listen. Listen to what is inside of you."

Her voice sounded like a dream voice, as if she was remembering a long-ago time. She closed her eyes, and I could tell by her loud breathing that she'd fallen asleep.

I wanted to work on my beading, to try making a curvy line, but the sewing things were in the kitchen, and the floor was wet. Even if I tiptoed across it, Kahasi would wake up and scold me. She liked the kitchen floor to sparkle, and it wouldn't sparkle if

I left tiptoe prints. I covered her with a blanket, then I just sat and watched her sleeping. Her mouth hung open a little, and her face looked as droopy as a wet cloth. She looked old when she was sleeping but young when she was awake. It was strange to see her hands not busy. Then she made a snorting sound and woke herself up.

"Did you have a good sleep?" I teased.

"Nah, I wasn't sleeping. I was just resting my eyes." She sat up a little straighter in her chair and tucked the blanket around her. "Did you go to Sequoia today?"

"No. Someone from the drug and alcohol center was going to be there to talk about addictions. He likes to have the little ones there so it feels more like a family gathering. They didn't need me to look after the babies, and I don't have any addictions, so I came here instead. Besides, the sweet grass he burns in the smudge makes me sneeze." Smudging – burning sage and sweet grass – is a cleansing ceremony. The sage rids a person of bad feelings, such as anger, while sweet grass brings positive energy.

"They smudge at school? When I went to school, we would have been punished for burning *sipaattsimaan*. It wasn't allowed, you know? None of our ways was allowed."

"But that was a long time ago. Things are different now. The new ways are better."

"Yes, my girl, sometimes the new ways are better." She closed her eyes again, breathed deeply a few times, then opened them slowly. "In the olden times, we would always smudge before the elders told a story. Did I ever tell you the story about White Buffalo Calf Woman?"

"No, will you tell me?"

She nodded and leaned forward in her chair. "This is the story of why the white buffalo is a sacred animal. This happened a long, long time ago, when the buffalo still walked on the prairie in great herds. It was getting to be the time of the year when the leaves turn yellow and fall off the trees. It was the time to hunt and to get food for the winter.

"Two hunters were sent as scouts to find out where the buffalo were walking. Even though they stood on the top of hills, they couldn't see the buffalo anywhere around. They looked and looked, but they saw nothing. Then one of the hunters saw some movement coming towards them. It looked like a lone young buffalo. It would be unusual for one buffalo to travel alone, especially a young one. Also, the color of this buffalo was wrong. It was not brown. It was as white as the snow in the wintertime. The men stared at the white buffalo calf." Kahasi's eyes grew round as she said this, and she held her hands open in front of her.

"The hunters were scared of this animal that kept coming

to them. They had never seen a buffalo like this one. When it got closer, the white buffalo blurred, as if a wind had pushed its spirit. The hunters could not believe their eyes – standing in front of them was not the white buffalo calf anymore, but a beautiful young woman. She was dressed in white buckskin. She was the most beautiful woman either of them had ever seen.

"One of the hunters said, 'I want to have that woman for a wife. I will go to that woman and take her in my arms.'

"The other hunter said, no, he must not do this, he must show her respect. But the first hunter did not listen. When he reached for the woman, there was a bad cloud, and when the cloud went away, all that was left of that hunter was a pile of bones.

"The hunter who was still alive started to pray. He knew this woman was sacred, a holy woman. When she spoke, he listened carefully. She said to him to go back to the camp and prepare for her. She said she would come to his people in four days, and she would bring a gift.

"He did these things, and in four days she came. She was carrying a bundle in her arms as if it were a baby. Inside the bundle was not a baby. It was a special pipe.

"The people were sorry they did not have any meat to share with the holy woman, but they dipped some sweet grass into a skin bag of water and gave it to her. To this day, we dip sweet grass or an eagle feather in water and sprinkle it on a person to purify them.

"The White Buffalo Calf Woman showed the people how to pray – the right words to use and the right gestures. She taught them that they are a living prayer, a bridge between the earth and the universe. She taught them many things, and then she left, saying she would come back to them someday. She walked away from the camp, and while she was walking away, the people saw her turn into four different colors of buffalo. The last one was a white female buffalo calf that disappeared over the horizon.

"A white buffalo calf is a very sacred animal. When a white buffalo calf comes, it will mean a time of healing, a time of peace. They say that she will bring harmony to the earth and prosperity to our people. But the old ones told us that we will not prosper until we have peace with all our enemies." Kahasi sat back in her chair. She had the dream-world look on her face again, but she didn't close her eyes. I think she was still seeing the White Buffalo Calf Woman. I could see her too – so beautiful, and carrying that bundle like a baby.

"That was a good story. Why did you tell it?"

"I have heard, me, that a white buffalo has been born. I have heard that it is at the Calgary Zoo. What is coming is a time of peace, when all people will work together in harmony and help each other," she said. "I would, me, like to see that white buffalo calf."

"Me too. Hey, maybe sometime when Dad is going to Calgary to play at a party, he could go to the zoo and take a picture for you."

"No, that would not be the same thing. I would like to feel the animal's spirit. I would like to feel the peace it will bring. I think, me, I will have to make that journey."

## Chapter 9

# A Letter for Lacey

"Ah, Lacey," sang Lila, waving a long white envelope and patting me on the shoulder. "I have something for you."

I shut off the tap that was filling the watering can and wiped my hands on my jeans. My plants were growing so big and strong now that they needed a lot more than just a mist of water. Between looking after the plants and babies, and being so busy at home, I'd almost forgotten the letter I'd sent offering to help the African grandmothers. I took the letter from Lila's hand. "Miss Lacey Little Bird, c/o Sequoia Outreach School, Gleichen, Alberta" was typed on a label on the front. I had never received a letter in the mail before. I was excited to open it, but I was also scared. What if they said, "No thank you, we don't need your

68

help"? That would make me feel terrible inside. What if they said, "Yes, hurry up, sew some purses, we need all the help we can get"? Between school and Sequoia and helping to look after Kayden and my little brothers, how could I find time to sew purses? And where did I think I was going to get the materials? The fabric? The thread? The sewing machine? Even if I got a sewing machine, what if I couldn't learn to run it? Who would teach me? A "yes please" answer was going to be worse than a "no thank you" answer. Why had I written the letter in the first place? Who did I think I was?

"Well," said Lila, standing with her hands on her hips, "are you going to just stand there staring at it, or are you going to open it?"

My heart was pounding because I didn't know whether I wanted the "yes" or the "no." Either one would be bad. I looked at Lila over the top of my glasses and picked at the flap. A small piece came off. I stuck my finger in the hole and ripped it along the edge. I lifted out the letter and unfolded it. It said:

Dear Miss Little Bird,

Thank you for your offer to help the Grandmothers to Grandmothers campaign by beginning a group in your community. We would be delighted if you could help us

— and the African grandmothers — in any way. We would appreciate any help you could offer.

I believe you live not far from Calgary. May I suggest that you send your purses to the Calgary Chapter? Your items could be added to its annual sale. As you know, all proceeds from the sale of the purses will be used to help grandmothers in Africa who are raising their grandchildren.

Also, I would like your permission to print the letter you sent to us in the official report we are preparing for the Grandmothers Gathering in Canada as an example of the different ways that Canadians are becoming involved with this campaign. The report will be distributed across the country. Please contact me as soon as possible to let me know if this would be all right with you. (You may do this by e-mail if you like. My address is at the top of this letter.)

Again, I would like to thank you for your work.

Warmly,
Maria Gonzales
Grandmothers to Grandmothers Campaign

I read the words, and my heart pounded even harder. The grandmothers had said yes! I couldn't believe it. I, Lacey Little

Bird from the Siksika First Nation, was going to be able to help the faraway grandmothers. I was going to help save lives.

Lila was tapping her foot. "Well?"

"They said yes, Lila. They said yes! Can you believe it? They said *yes!*"

She smiled. "I can believe it," she said. "I'm very, very proud of you, young lady. Your heart is surely in the right place." She wrapped me in her warm, jiggly arms.

I skipped into the kitchen, where Mrs. B. was pouring a cup of coffee. "Mrs. B! The grandmothers said yes! And they want to use my letter in some kind of report. Isn't this great?"

Mrs. Buchanan smiled. "Congratulations, Lacey. I know you'll do a great job."

"But they want me to take the purses to a sale in Calgary. How am I going to get them there?"

"Let's worry about that once you've made some. I'm sure we'll find a way."

I was so full of excitement I felt like I might burst. I wished Angel were at school so I could tell her. I wished I could run all the way to Kahasi's house to tell her, and all the way to my house so I could tell Mum. I wanted everyone to know the good news. And I wanted to get started right away.

But – I had a few problems. First, I didn't have any fabric. Maybe I could cut up some old clothes, the way Angel had done.

But people had to buy these purses. Would anyone pay money for purses made from old, worn-out clothes? I didn't think so.

My eyes wandered around Sequoia as I was thinking. I spotted the boxes of donated clothes and baby things that were free for the taking. Maybe there was some fabric in there. If there was, maybe I would be allowed to have it. I was so anxious to get going that I forgot to be shy. I walked right up to Mrs. B. and blurted, "Do you have any material I could use to make purses?"

"I'm sure you'll be able to find some things here to get started. You are welcome to look through our craft supplies and use what you need. But for now, aren't you supposed to be looking after some babies?"

There were only three babies at Sequoia that afternoon, but all of them were awake. I laid the smallest one on his back on a blanket so he could get stronger by kicking his legs and waving his arms – when I made a funny face at him or tickled him, he'd kick with happiness. I sat another baby up on the blanket and rolled a ball to her. The third one I kept in my lap. I was hoping they would get tired really quickly, so I could go through that box of donated material, but the babies kept having fun. It was hard to look after them when I wanted to do something else. Eventually I put each of them into a baby seat on the floor and dragged the box over; they could have fun watching me having fun.

The box of material reminded me of Kahasi's basket, except the pieces were bigger. I found a length of shiny gold material that felt as soft as a baby's skin when I rubbed it against my face, and some material printed with bright sunflowers. There was gold thread in the box, too.

"Yes, you may have those," said Mrs. B. when I asked. "I'll be interested to see the purses you make."

Now I had to learn more about making purses. Angel had been happy when she had found the part of the denim purse the elf had stitched together by hand. She had guessed right away that I was the elf. The bag to carry Kayden's diapers and toys turned out all right, but it took a long time. If I was going to help the grandmothers, I would have to learn to sew much faster. Kahasi was right – I would need a sewing machine. But where was I going to find a sewing machine in a place where everyone liked to sew by hand? And even if I found a machine, who would teach me how to use it?

I thought of these problems all of the next day, even when I was supposed to be doing other things. In social studies class, Mrs. Martinez's purse that looked like a quilt was sitting on the floor by her desk. All during the class I kept looking at that purse. I was thinking about the African grandmothers, and the parents dying of AIDS, and their little children. I thought about Angel and Kayden. I thought about how I had spoken to Mrs. B. and asked to help the grandmothers, and how it hadn't been too hard to do. But this was Mrs. Martinez, not Mrs. B., and this was not Sequoia. What if Mrs. Martinez told me I was stupid? Or what if she told the class, and they all laughed at me?

"Lacey? Are you paying attention?" Mrs. Martinez asked, and everyone looked at me. I felt ashamed and stared down at my desk. I didn't say anything.

I didn't hear much of what she said for the rest of the class either, but I tried to look like I was paying attention. I closed my book slowly when the bell rang. I had to talk to her. I had to do it for the grandmothers. Knowing that the grandmothers needed me gave me strength.

Mrs. Martinez couldn't see me moving slowing, gathering up my nerve. She was wiping off the words she had written on the whiteboard. My arms were filled with books, but I tapped her arm.

"Yes, Lacey," she said. She smiled a big, kind smile. I guess she wasn't still mad at me for daydreaming.

"Mrs. Martinez, I noticed you had a really nice purse, made like a quilt."

"Do you like that old thing?" she asked, then laughed softly. "I've had that for years and years. I made it a long time ago. I wanted to make a memory quilt, but it was taking me too long." She picked up the purse from the floor. It was simply made, a bit like Angel's bag, but the pieces were smaller and more colorful, like birds in a faraway place. They all had a fancy embroidery stitch around the edges.

"Each piece of fabric has a special memory. This one is the oldest," she said, pointing to a shiny, white piece. "It's from my mother's wedding dress. This is from my graduation dress, and *this* piece is from my favorite pair of jeans – the ones that fell apart because I wore them so much."

"*Matsowa'p*," I said, without thinking. Kahasi had told me that in the old days children were punished for speaking Blackfoot at school, but Mrs. Martinez just smiled at me.

"What does that mean?" she asked.

"It means it's beautiful," I said. "I like how all the colors don't match, but go together anyway."

"Me too," she said. "That's why I wanted to make a quilt. I thought it would be pretty. I also thought it would be like sleeping under all these memories. But I'm very slow at sewing by hand, and some of the pieces – like this bit from the edge of a blanket I loved when I was a baby – are so small. I'm kind of impatient, so I used a sewing machine in the end, and made a big purse instead of a quilt."

"My grandmother tells me I'm impatient, too." I smiled a

bit, but kept my lips covering my teeth. I could feel the grand-mothers nudging me to ask what I really wanted to ask. "Do you think...do you think you would mind showing me sometime how to use a sewing machine?"

"Well..." Mrs. Martinez twisted her mouth as if she was try-ing to slow down the words before they came out. "I can't exactly do that."

My heart fell, but I lifted my eyebrows to ask why without seeming rude.

"The truth is, this bag is the only thing I've ever sewn. When I was done, I decided I'd never, ever try to sew again. I just hate sewing with all my heart. I'm afraid it's one thing I simply can-not teach."

My heart started beating wildly again. Maybe Mrs. Martinez still had a sewing machine she didn't want. I didn't know what words to use to ask her about it. I ran my fingers gently over the hand-stitching she'd done on the edge of each piece.

"Do you still have that machine?" My voice rushed ahead of me, saying all the things that were in my head. "You see, I want to make purses to help some grandmothers in Africa, but I need to make a lot. I need a sewing machine to do that. Could I borrow yours, maybe? I'd take special care of it and make sure my brothers didn't ever touch it. Ever. I could bring it back to you whenever you wanted it."

Mrs. Martinez's mouth twisted again, as if she was thinking, as if she didn't want to tell me something. My heart and my hopes fell.

"It's OK," I said. "I understand. I probably wouldn't want to lend my sewing machine, either."

"No, Lacey, that's not it," she said, touching my arm. "If I had a sewing machine, I'd lend it to you and teach you what I know, but I don't have one. I used my mother's machine, and she lives way off in Manitoba. I'm sorry."

"That's OK. I'll think of something else," I said.

But what was I saying? What was there to think of? I didn't know anyone – even Kahasi, who knew everyone, didn't know anyone – with a sewing machine. I wished those African grandmothers hadn't said yes. I had to do those purses, especially since they were putting my letter in their report. But how? How was I going to do it?

## Chapter 10

# Kahasi's Big Surprise

I was starting to get worried about Mum. She seemed to be getting sicker and sicker, and she wouldn't let us tell Dad when he phoned. Most days, she was lying on the sofa watching soap operas or snoozing when I got home from Sequoia. When she was awake, she seemed to have a lot of pain in the middle of her back. Angel had started taking the early bus home at two o'clock so she could practice her nursing on Mum. She would rub her back and help her get washed and dressed. Auntie Michelle would bring my youngest brothers, Davis and Colton, back from her place where they spent most of the day playing with their cousins. My other brothers came home on the later school bus with me.

I was spending so much time looking after Kayden that I was starting to think I was her mother, not her auntie. This was a bad thing because I didn't want to be anybody's mother. I liked it better when Angel had time to be the mother, and I had time to spend with Kahasi. I missed being able to visit her every day and having time to sew.

Dad and my oldest brother, Liland, were usually the cooks at our house, but when they were on the road with the band, it was mostly my job. I liked cooking when I helped Dad and when I helped Lila at Sequoia, but it wasn't much fun being stuck in the kitchen by myself. Usually I made spaghetti or scrambled eggs, because those were the things I could make best. Tonight, though, I was going to make fry-bread tacos because I thought they might make Mum feel better. I had asked Kahasi to come over so she could tell me how to do it.

Thinking of my grandmother coming to visit made me happy. I missed my dad less when I could spend time with her. I hadn't seen her for a few days, because I had been so busy with school and Kayden and cooking. Soon our quiet times together would be over. Already cardboard boxes were appearing at Kahasi's house. She was going to stay with Uncle Douglas and Auntie Michelle.

Kahasi was sitting at the kitchen table showing me how to mix the flour, baking powder, and water with a fork to make the dough for the fry bread. She showed me how to stretch the balls into flat circles, and dimple the edges with my thumb and fingers. Flour was everywhere – over the table, on the floor, on my shirt, even on her face. I reached over to wipe a spray of flour from her cheek, but I made it worse. Now there were pieces of dough there, too. "You look so funny!" I laughed.

Kahasi reached over and stuck some sticky dough on my nose. She laughed. "Now we are twins. You look funny, too."

It was easy to see which pieces of fry bread were the ones I had made and which were the pieces my grandmother had made. Hers were so perfect they looked as if they had been made by a machine. Mine were all different shapes, and some had holes in them. "Don't worry how they look, they will all taste the same," she said.

We kept busy, making lots of fry bread so we would have some left over. As her hands worked quickly to make the circles, Kahasi told me, "I have something I think you will like, Lacey. It is something of your father's from long ago. I think it is something you should have."

I looked at her expectantly, thinking she'd take the gift out of her pocket.

"It was too heavy for me to carry. When your dad comes, he can bring it to you."

"But Dad's not going to be home for days yet. Can't you tell me what it is?"

"It is something old and maybe broken," she said. "But, like most things, not so broken it can't be fixed."

Who would want something old and broken? "What is it? Please tell me." Her riddle was making me crazy. But she must not have heard my question.

"It doesn't seem to have any rust," she added. "We found it in the basement when your uncles were moving my things. It must have been there a long time. I had forgotten all about it. Your father, too, maybe."

"What *is* it?" I asked again.

"You come home with me to Uncle Douglas's, and I will show you."

It was a good thing Kahasi was moving in with family. She had gone deaf, I was sure of it. I didn't bother to ask again. Even if she heard me, she would just tell me to practice my patience and wait.

I tried to think of what the present might be as I stirred the hamburger in the big frying pan. When I heard the sound of tires on gravel, I glanced out the window above the sink. It was Uncle Douglas's green van! Dad waved wildly out the window when he saw me, then reached over and honked the horn, "Beep! Beep! Beep, beep, beep!" "It's Dad!" I yelled. "Dad's home!"

I rushed from the kitchen and down the stairs so I could be at the front of the stampede. I wanted to be the first to hug Dad. I was so happy to see him that I started to cry. He lifted me up as if I were little. "How's my princess?" he laughed, as he swung me in a circle. When he set me down, he was dusted with flour from my shirt. My brothers had flooded out of the house and surrounded Dad and me. The little boys pushed and wormed their way to him. Auntie Michelle came running from her house to clutch Uncle Douglas in a hug. All of his kids mobbed him, too. The side door of the van slid open, and Liland and Jack crawled from the back seat. By now, Kahasi had come out of the house, and Angel had brought Mum. After he hugged his mother and Angel, Dad drew Mum into the biggest hug of all, and kissed her.

Liland and Jack gave high-fives to all their brothers, then pulled open the back doors of the van. Piled on top of the guitars, drums, and amps were bags and bags of groceries. It looked like enough food to feed an army.

Dad kept his arm wrapped around Mum's waist as they

walked to the house. Davis, my smallest brother, held my dad's other hand. "You coming in?" Dad called to Uncle Douglas.

"No, I think I'll let these kids carry me home. We'll come over a bit later, so I can correct all your stories," said Uncle Douglas.

Making the fry-bread tacos with my dad and Kahasi and all my family around was one of the happiest times of my life. It didn't even bother me that Kelvin was there. Dad and my big brothers kept smiling as they told stories about being on the road, and how the people in one town liked the band so much that they asked them to play for ten days straight. "We're rich, by the way," Dad laughed. "At least, we were rich until we stopped at the grocery store!"

It was a noisy night at our house. There were stories and laughter and singing, and as much happiness and love as there possibly can be in one house.

By the time the darkness started to come, Kahasi said to Dad, "I am tired now. Perhaps, my son, you would take this old woman home to rest?"

"Of course, Mum. Of course," he said, letting go of my mum's hand.

"Lacey, maybe you could help too," she said to me. She gave me a big wink with her left eye, and I remembered the surprise she'd promised. The three of us went to my uncle's house.

"It's up here, in my room," said Kahasi. She opened the door of her closet.

"A sewing machine?" I exclaimed. "A sewing machine! You found a sewing machine?"

"It was back there at my old house all the time. Hidden in the basement." She smiled. "Sometimes old women forget about things."

"I can't believe it," said Dad, lifting the machine from the closet. "I bet this thing hasn't been used for twenty years. Remember I used to use it when I started dancing – to make traditional outfits? I had so much fun with this machine. I don't know why I ever stopped sewing."

"Perhaps the machine stopped sewing," suggested Kahasi. "I don't know if it works."

"Well, that should be easy enough to figure out. We'll plug it in and see. And if it doesn't work, we'll get Kelvin to have a look. He can fix anything with a motor." He said these words with pride in his voice. How could he be proud of Kelvin? I didn't want that creep touching the sewing machine.

Dad kissed his mother on the cheek and wished her good night. I gave her a kiss too, and a hug. "You're the best, Kahasi. You're the best," I told her. She smiled at me, took my hand, and didn't let go.

"Talk to your father, Lacey. Tell him your troubles," she said.

Then she called after me, "Be careful, you. Don't be getting better at sewing than I am. Old women have pride, too, you know."

I kept smiling as we walked from Uncle Douglas's house to our house through the cool darkness of night, with Dad carrying the sewing machine. I wanted to tell him about all the terrible things that had happened while he was gone, but I was afraid of spoiling his homecoming. He seemed so happy that I pushed the difficult things from my mind.

"This was yours, Dad? I can't believe you never told me you could sew."

"Well, my girl, I guess you never asked. Besides, I didn't know you had such an interest," he said. "You've been busy while I've been gone. I'll be anxious to have a look at your beading."

That was when I remembered that he didn't know yet about the African grandmothers or the letter I had sent, so I told him about it. He also didn't know about Kelvin and Angel's problems, but I didn't tell him that.

"That's quite an offer you've made, Lacey, very generous," he said. His smile told me he was proud. "But do you really think you can do it? After all, you're just beginning to sew. To raise enough money to make a difference, you're going to have to sew – and sell – a lot of purses."

"With a machine, I'm sure I can do it," I said, but I wasn't really as confident as my words. If Dad wasn't sure, how could I be? What if it turned out that I was bad at sewing with a machine? What if no one had money to buy the purses? What then? I pushed thoughts of failing from my mind. Instead I asked, "Will you teach me?"

"Once we clean it up – and if this thing runs – I'll start teaching you tomorrow," he said. He put a plastic bag on the floor beside my bed, then put the machine down on it, so it would be the first thing I saw in the morning.

"Now," he said, "off to bed with you. Go say good night to everyone, then crawl under the covers. There's school tomorrow and sewing lessons after school. Be gone!"

I wrapped my arms around him in a tight hug. "I love you, Dad," I said.

"I love you too, my daughter." He slipped his hand into his pocket on his way out the door. "Oh, I almost forgot," he said, pulling out a small packet of sunflower seeds. "I bought these for you, for your gardening project. They grow really fast, and they have happy faces just like yours. How are your plants growing, anyway? No, don't tell me." He held up his hand to stop my words. "We'll save that for tomorrow." He shut off the light and closed the door on the sounds of people talking in the kitchen.

Tomorrow. Tomorrow, when we were alone, I would tell Dad everything.

Chapter 11

# The Lesson

The smell of stew simmering on the stove greeted me when I opened the door of my house after school. It was so good to have Dad home. The first thing I saw was the sewing machine on the kitchen table. Dad had cleaned it up so it looked almost new. It was a color between white and yellow, and had a few knobs on the front and a big wheel on one side.

Giggling voices came from the basement, so I guessed Dad was there with my little brothers. I started to go down the steps. "Where are you heading off to?" asked Dad, coming down the hall. "Don't we have a date?"

My big smile said yes.

"Come on then. Into the kitchen with you. I cleaned the

machine up, and Kelvin oiled it. It seems to work just fine." I winced at Kelvin's name; it reminded me that I had to talk to Dad about him. "Sit here, in front of the machine," Dad said.

He took a spool of thread from the table and put it on a sticklike thing on top of the machine. "Now, watch carefully," he said. He pulled the thread and wound it slowly through the metal loops and knobs until it snaked to the needle. The eye of the needle was at the bottom, not at the top like on regular needles. He pulled the thread under a little flat part he called the foot, and fished another thread from the bottom part of the machine.

"You use two threads?"

"Uh-huh."

He pressed a switch on the machine, and a light shone on the area near the foot. "You see that box on the floor? That's the pedal. It's what gives the machine power. You press it just like the gas pedal of a car. You push just a little if you want to go slowly."

I put two pieces of fabric together the way he showed me, dropped the foot of the machine in place, and pressed the pedal with my foot. It made a humming sound as if it wanted to start, but nothing moved. I looked up at Dad.

"Press a little harder," he said.

I pushed my foot down on the pedal. The humming stopped,

but the needle punched up and down furiously, pulling the fabric from my hands.

"Dad! Help!" I yelled as the machine sucked in the fabric. "It's going by itself!"

"Take your foot off the pedal."

Learning to use the machine was tricky at first.

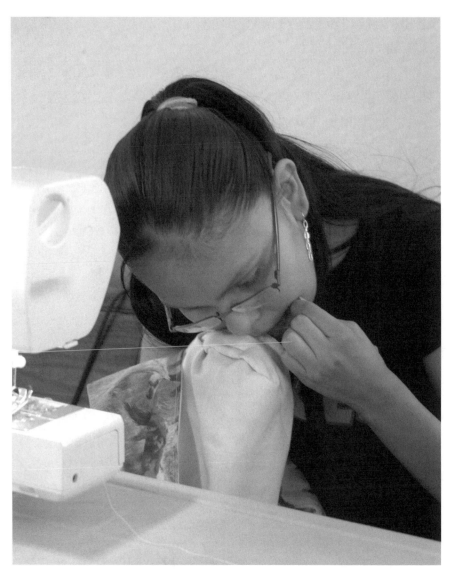

With a little patience and practice, sewing became much easier.

I did, and the machine stopped immediately. Dad released the foot of the machine and showed me what I had sewn. The line of stitching was crooked and bunched up in places.

"OK, so..." he said, "I guess I need to tell you a few other things." He showed me how to use the dials on the front of the machine to adjust the tension of the thread, to keep it from bunching up, and the little marks on the machine where I needed to line things up to get a straight seam. "You'll catch on with a little practice," he said. He also showed me how to rip out a seam that wasn't right.

The machine sewed quickly, but what use was it if it didn't do a good job? If I was going to spend my time ripping out seams, I might as well do the sewing by hand.

"You'll get the hang of it. It's all about tension and control. Tension with the thread and control with the speed. It just takes patience."

Great, I thought, patience again. The one thing I was short on, I seemed to need the most.

Dad ripped out the rest of the seam for me and passed me the pieces. The machine was slowly pecking up and down when the phone rang.

"Hello," said Dad. "Oh, hi! Yes. Yah. Uh-huh. Tonight?" He looked at the clock on the stove. "That doesn't give us much time. Dang it, that's too bad. I'd like to help you, but – Sure.

Sure. It'll take us an hour to get there and then to set up, but I suppose we could do it. The van is still loaded, and as long as you don't mind if we start a bit late."

I didn't like the sound of this conversation. Red Lightning must be going back on the road. Tonight, he'd said. *Tonight.*

Dad hung up the phone. I looked at him expectantly.

"I guess your brothers and uncle and I are back on the road. But it's just for a couple of days. The band they had booked cancelled at the last minute, when the singer got laryngitis."

"But you just got home, Dad," I complained.

"I know, honey. I won't be gone long."

He picked up the phone to call Uncle Douglas, went to talk with Mum, and called downstairs to Liland and Jack, "Time to pack up. Come on, let's go." I know he hated to leave so soon, but he also sounded excited that people needed him to sing and play his guitar.

It seemed just minutes before Dad, Liland, Jack, and Uncle Douglas threw their duffel bags into the van and drove off. They didn't even take the time to eat the stew Dad had made. And I hadn't found the time to talk to Dad about all the things that were troubling me.

## Chapter 12

# The Blow-up

My younger brothers were asleep in their beds when Angel, carrying Kayden, slumped onto the sofa. It was technically past my bedtime, but it was Saturday, Dad was still away on that emergency trip, and Mum was in her bedroom.

"Mum sick again?" I asked from behind my sewing machine.

"She's been throwing up again, and she has a real bad headache. She's in bed, trying to get some sleep," said Angel, not even looking up from her magazine. Kayden was on the sofa beside her. "Pretty. Pretty lady," she said to Kayden, pointing to the pictures. "Dog. See the doggie? Woof. Woof." Kayden batted the magazine with her hand and slobbered like a dog. Angel turned another page. "Oh, shoes. Nice shoes. Pretty shoes. Purple. Look at the pretty purple shoes. Mommy would like to have those shoes. Pretty. Would Kayden like some pretty shoes?"

I wished she would shut up. The gold fabric I had cut out was slippery and hard to keep together. The thread from the bobbin kept tangling in a heap and puckering the fabric.

"Kitty cat. That's a kitty cat. Pat the kitty. Nice kitty. 'Meow,' says the kitty," said Angel. I sighed loudly and snipped carefully at the mass of threads.

"Angel? Angel? Are you there?" came Mum's faint voice from the next room.

"Mum is calling you, Angel," I said, relieved I wouldn't have to listen to the baby talk.

"I'll be right back. Watch Kayden, OK?"

"Uh-huh." I glanced at Kayden. She was safely holding onto the sofa and slapping it with one hand. She had a homemade rattle filled with rice in her other hand. I turned back to my sewing. Every time I got everything in place, it would slide away. I stuck in pins and more pins, trying to get it to all hold together. I slid the piece beneath the foot of the machine and started the line of stitching. The machine helped drown out the annoying ticka-ticka-ticka of Kayden's rattle, but I could still hear it, so I knew she was fine. As the machine pecked slowly at the fabric, I glanced over to check on her. She was smiling so happily that I could see her two bottom teeth.

"Ga!" she said.

*Crunch!* The machine's needle hit a pin and snapped cleanly in two.

"Arghh! I hate sewing," I growled, as I cut the thread and loosened the bolt to the needle. I hoped there was a spare needle in the small box of extra parts Dad had put in my sewing box. If not, I wouldn't be able to get another one until someone went to the city. But when I reached down, my sewing basket wasn't beside me. Spools of my white and black thread were unraveled all over the living room floor. Appliques, badges, and hundreds of beads were scattered everywhere. Kayden was plunked on the floor beside the sewing basket, clutching a plastic case with pins inside.

"Kayden! You stupid, stupid baby!" I shouted as I jumped up. The shiny fabric slithered to the floor, and the chair banged backwards as I ran to her. I grabbed her pudgy arm and pried the case of pins from her strong fingers. It wasn't her rattle I had been hearing; it was my pins.

"You're a brat, Kayden. Just a stupid brat!" I screamed. She stopped smiling and gurgling. Her bottom lip trembled, and her eyes filled with tears as I lifted her from the floor.

Angel walked into the room and shrieked. "Don't call her that! She isn't stupid, and she isn't a brat!"

"Look what she did! Just look!"

"You're the stupid one, leaving stuff everywhere," Angel said, pulling her crying baby to her chest. "It's OK, Kayden. You're smart. Really, really smart," she said quietly, but loud enough for me to hear. "It's Lacey who's stupid, leaving her things where your little hands can get them. She's so stupid she thinks she can help people in Africa. She can't even help people in her own family when they need their baby watched for a few minutes."

"I shouldn't have to watch your stupid baby. She's yours. Not mine!"

Joseph and Davis came out of their room, Davis wearing his Scooby-Doo pajamas and Joseph in his boxers. Their eyes were puffy from sleeping. "What's going on?" asked Joseph. "We heard yelling, and Davis was scared."

Kayden had been soothed by the sound of Angel's voice and her gentle jiggling. She stopped crying. "Nothing important is going on," Angel said. "Come on, boys, back to bed. I'll tuck you in." I glared at her back as she left the room talking sweetly to all three children. She turned and stuck her tongue out at me, and Kayden laughed.

I swept the beads into the small tin that Kahasi had given me, and stuffed my sewing things into the basket. I could feel tears filling my eyes.

What if Angel was right? What if I was stupid to try to help the African women? What if I couldn't learn to sew? What if I wasn't smart and talented like my dad? What was I going to do then?

# Changes

Dad came home after a few days, which was a huge relief. It took a few weeks for things to settle back to normal, but I felt happy again, and good things had started to happen. Unfortunately, Kelvin was still Angel's boyfriend, but he wasn't at Sequoia much. He was still mad about having to take math over again, so he hardly ever showed up for anything. I thought he should get Angel to help him, since she was good in math, but – as usual – he didn't like my ideas.

When he wasn't holding Angel's hand or hugging her – which just made me feel sick – he was just as mean as ever. He spent most of his time at the gas station across the street from Sequoia, mostly just hanging around. That had been Dad's idea.

Dad figured if Kelvin could make himself useful, maybe he could get a job there, maybe apprentice. But Dad also wanted Kelvin to finish school. I don't think the man who owned the garage liked the idea of letting someone who had stolen a car and had a criminal record work for him. He probably wasn't even crazy about having a thief there at all, but sometimes Kelvin would pump gas, sweep out the garage, pass tools to the mechanic, and pretend he was useful.

That was the bad part – that Kelvin was still around. The good parts were that the sewing machine was working better for me now, Mum had gone to have that operation and was feeling much better, Dad was home more often, and those plants I had been watering every single day weren't so little anymore. They had grown way too tall for the containers with plastic lids.

Lila, Mrs. B., and Trisha had helped me re-plant them into some old flowerpots Lila had gathered from people she knew. We stuffed lots of plants into each pot, but we had to be careful doing it so the roots weren't disturbed. Mrs. B. said it was best if the plants didn't realize they had been moved into new pots. We had put some of them up on the window ledges, so they'd get more sunlight and grow better. Every couple of days I switched the containers around, so all of the plants would have the same chance to grow. It was a lot more work than when they were little – when I just had to spray them with water. And since Sequoia is in a basement and the windows are near the ceiling, it meant I had to climb on a chair now to water them. The water was heavy to lift that high, and they sure drank a lot of water.

Some of the plants were as tall as my forearm was long, and the leaves had gotten as round as the palm of my hand. Some of them even had swollen buds with color peeking out. I was curious to see if the red flower or the yellow flower would be the first one to bloom. I also wanted to eat one, but I knew I wouldn't eat the first ones to bloom. For that, I would have to be patient.

With all of the waiting I had to do with everything, I was getting to be more patient. But still, it would be great when the nasturtiums bloomed, and even better when we could put them outside for everyone to see. But even though there were leaves on the tress now, Mrs. B. said it wouldn't be warm enough for the nasturtiums to go outside until after Easter Break. That meant at least two more weeks of waiting, waiting, waiting.

By the time Easter was over, the days were getting longer, and the sun was getting so warm each afternoon that I didn't need to wear my jacket on my way from my school to Sequoia. I skipped down the street, feeling the warm sun on my skin. I was hoping it was time to put all those flowerpots outside to make the town look prettier, but even more, I wanted to see how the plants looked. I'd been worried about them all during the school holidays. I wondered how they would survive for ten days with only the water in their saucers. Angel had promised me she'd water the plants when she got to school that morning, but I didn't know if she had remembered to do it. I was also anxious to see the flowers. They hadn't bothered to open before the school break.

"Ah, Lacey. I've been waiting for you." Mrs. B. had a big smile on her face as she walked across the room to meet me. "We have a surprise for you."

I wanted to see the surprise, but I wanted to see my plants more. I gave her my shy smile and didn't say anything.

"Come on," she said, putting her arm lightly on my back and directing me to the stairs. "The surprise is outside."

All of my plants were there. Thirteen pots in all different sizes and shapes. Some were made of plastic, and some were made of clay. Some of the pots were hanging by wires from the tree, and some were beside the sidewalk. The plants were so bushy that you couldn't tell that the tops of some of the pots were chipped. The plants had their leaves turned to the south, to the sunshine. My face smiled the big smile now, the one that shows my crooked teeth.

"They look beautiful," I said. I bent close to the blue pot.

Some of the flowers were almost hidden by the big leaves, but I could see that they were shaped like a cone with a flared end.

"The boys carried them outside this afternoon, and Lila set them up," said Mrs. B. "They really are stunning, and they make the whole street look brighter. There is one more pot to bring out. It will go on the front steps of the church, but I told them to wait. I wanted you to see all of these first."

I felt so proud of my flowers and how they looked. I felt as if the sun was shining from me. I had made this beauty with my own hands. Everything seemed to be perfect.

Chapter 14

# Heartbreak

The weather in Alberta in the springtime is a crazy thing. Some days it's as hot as summer, some days it's as cold as fall, and some days the wind blows so hard it feels as if it will knock you over.

Clouds had covered the moon last night, and the wind that blew through my sweater made it feel colder than it had been since winter. I was worried that a frost might have come to hurt my flowers. I was supposed to cover them up with sheets after school, just in case a late frost came, but I'd been so busy yesterday that I forgot. I didn't like how that wind felt. I hoped my forgetfulness hadn't killed my plants. That would be a horrible thing to happen.

When the bus dropped me off at my school, I ran past the six houses to Sequoia, hoping to check on my plants and then run back to my own school before the bell rang. Besides, I wanted to see if Lila had made muffins. Dad was away again, and I didn't have time to eat breakfast or make my own lunch this morning. Mum wasn't up yet because she had been busy helping Angel take care of the baby. Kayden was sick and had been crying all night.

I glanced at the heavy clay pot on the front step; the plants were safe. They looked as green and lively as they had yesterday, and even more of the buds had burst into yellow, orange, and red flowers. I quickly counted them. Sixteen. Sixteen flowers in one pot! I leapt over the railing of the steps and spun to the side of the church, anxious to see if the other pots had as many blooms. My mouth dropped open. I couldn't believe what I saw.

Dirt and smashed pots and battered plants were strewn around everywhere. It looked as if someone had stomped on the plants and crushed them into the sidewalk. Branches were broken off the tree, too. Splinters of clear and colored glass sparkled on the ground – the middle window of the church was shattered, and beneath it was a smear of dirt and fragments of a flowerpot. Bad words were written on the wall of the church with black spray paint. Two of the basement windows had been kicked in.

"Who could do this? Who *would* do this?" I gasped. My hands made fists, and I wanted to hit something. I wanted to punch whoever had done this – punch them hard, right in the face, where it would hurt most. I wanted to beat up whoever had been so horribly mean to my plants and to me. I felt attacked, betrayed. I felt as if I didn't matter – no matter what I did or how hard I worked, someone would be there to destroy everything.

Then, looking at my poor plants, I felt tears in my eyes. I lifted a lifeless plant from the grass beneath the tree. Its red flower drooped sadly, as wilted and dead as a wildflower picked from the prairie. Frost hadn't killed my plants. Some wicked person had. Why would anyone do such a thing?

I shifted my glasses to wipe away the angry tears that were making everything blurry. I slung my backpack over my shoulder and cradled the wilted plant in my hands as gently as if it were a baby bird. Maybe, if it had some water, it would come back to life.

Just then, Lila came up behind me, carrying a garbage can and a broom. "Oh Lacey," she said. "I can't believe someone would do this. I am so sorry. I knew it was possible, but I didn't really think it would happen." The dead flowers brought tears to her eyes, too. She reached for me and tried to put her arms around me like a mother, but I shrugged off her touch.

"I *told* you this would happen! I told you someone would

wreck them. Now all my work was for nothing!" I didn't care that my words might hurt Lila. I wanted someone else to feel my pain, too. Instead of putting the plant in water, I clenched it in my fist and ran away.

"No, Lacey. Wait! We can repair the damage," I heard Lila call.

I ran blindly toward my school, then past it, and past the cemetery. I ran until I was panting and my left side felt as if it had a knife in it. I ran until there was nowhere left to run. I was at the edge of Gleichen, near the water tower, when I spotted the life-sized carving of a buffalo hidden partly by the spruce trees in the park. I felt drawn to the statue with its feet planted solidly on the ground. Its head was bent down and turned slightly, as if it was getting ready to charge an enemy. I knew how that buffalo felt; I wanted to charge, too.

I put my hand out to stroke the curly hair of its forehead. It was as cold and hard as the person who had ruined my flowers. "Why do people do these things?" I cried out loud to the sky. "I don't understand!" I stomped my feet and beat my arms up and down. "Why? Why? Why?"

Maybe Kelvin was right. Maybe it was true that nothing would ever change for our people. Maybe he wasn't poisoning Angel with his thoughts of failure – maybe he was right. Just plain right. Maybe changing things was hopeless. I wished I had lived a long time ago when things were simpler, when families were always together, and the only thing to worry about was how to hunt buffalo.

I let the tears drip down my cheeks as I slid down beside the buffalo's strong forelegs. My sadness shook me until I was tired and weak from the crying. I stayed there a long time and wished my dad was at home. I missed him more than ever. Everything seemed to go wrong when he was away. I sat there while the cold wind shifted around me and made me shiver. I ducked my neck as far into my jacket as I could and pulled my arms up the sleeves so I could wrap them around me inside. Still, I shivered.

What else could go wrong? My flowers were destroyed. I had yelled at Lila. I was late for school. I was hungry. There was no way for me to go home, and it was too far to walk. I was alone and scared, and I was out of choices.

I started back towards school, walking slowly with my hands in my pockets. The wind kept trying to push me backwards. I thought the wind might be right. Maybe I shouldn't hurry to get to school – I would be in trouble for being so late. I hoped the school secretary hadn't phoned my mum yet.

When the school bus dropped me off at my house at the end of the day, I raced to see my grandmother. Kahasi would listen. She would understand. My backpack thunked like a stone when it hit the floor. I told Kahasi what had happened to my plants.

"Why are they so mean? Why did they do this?" I was angry again as I told her the story. "I don't understand why they want to smash things and write bad words with spray paint. It doesn't make sense! I know it's people from Siksika doing this. But why, Kahasi? *Why?*"

My grandmother poured steaming water from the kettle into two cups. She dipped the tea bags up and down as she spoke.

"They feel helpless," she said quietly. "I think, me, the anger makes them feel brave and strong. Breaking things gives them power. It gives them something to do when they feel they can do nothing."

"But that's wrong! It's wrong to wreck things and hurt people!"

"You speak with a woman's wisdom, but you show me the anger of a man. Which one will be stronger, ah?"

She put the cups on the table and lifted a tea towel from a plate. I was so upset that I hadn't smelled the fry bread. I wanted to reach for a piece, but I was too furious.

"Anger is a terrible thing, my girl, and you are right, anger destroys." She lifted the tea bag from her cup and poured in milk from the can. "Anger makes other people afraid, too. Maybe afraid to try again." She stirred her tea slowly. "Come," she said, "eat. Food helps to calm anger. Maybe you'll feel better once you eat."

I didn't want to eat, but fry bread is my favorite food, and it looked delicious. My stomach rumbled so loudly that I thought she must have heard. I sat across the table from her and fixed my tea the way she fixed hers. Then I reached for a piece of the soft *immistsiihkiitaan*. I was surprised she didn't ask me the Blackfoot name the way she usually did. I chewed it slowly, then I reached for another piece. It was so quiet that I could hear the sound of my chewing, and the ticking clock. Kahasi picked up her sewing. She was finishing the edges of that quilt for my cousin.

"I haven't seen you much lately. I thought maybe you had a boyfriend." I knew she was teasing me. Her eyes sparkled, and she lifted an eyebrow. "Huh? You have a boyfriend? You getting married?"

"No, I don't have a boyfriend, but my plants took a lot of time. They were growing so well that I had to keep putting them into bigger and bigger pots, and then the boys put them outside to make the town look better. It did look better. It looked almost like a picture in a magazine. Now it's all gone. Wasted." I reached for my beading. I only had the center of the flower left to fill in with beads, then I'd be finished one of the uppers.

"Wasted? No, not wasted."

"Yes, it is! Everything. Everything was destroyed. All the flowerpots, all the plants. Even a window of the church."

"Tell me, did you like it when you made the plants grow? Did you like the smell of the earth?"

"Oh, yes! You should have seen them. They grew from these little curled-up seeds into plants that had leaves as big as cookies. And some of the plants had flowers. They looked so beautiful."

"Well then, nothing has been destroyed. The breaking of the pots can't take away how growing things made you feel. The only thing that has been hurt is your pride. You can grow new plants."

"I don't want to grow new plants. I want the old ones back."

"But you told me the old ones are destroyed. Gone. What is left of the old plants is your memory of them and how they made you feel. You know how to grow more. It was a bad thing that happened, but it can be fixed. Making things right is up to you."

I didn't understand why I should have to fix something that someone else ruined. Whoever ruined it should have to fix it.

Kahasi hummed to herself as she sewed. She hummed an old song that had no words. I stretched my lips around my teeth as I concentrated on making small, tight stitches that would be invisible. I was getting better at beading, but it was hard to get the beads to fit into the tight spiral of the center, harder than I had expected. I had to be careful to get it right. Lots of times, I had to take out stitches and start again. I hated doing things over, but when I did, they sometimes turned out better.

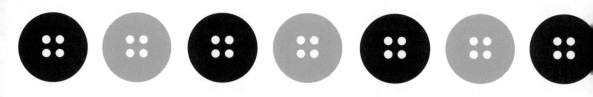

# Showdown

I could hear Kelvin's angry voice spitting hateful words, and I could hear Angel crying as soon as I stepped through the door. "Stop it! Stop it!" I called as I ran up the stairs to the kitchen.

Kelvin's eyes were black and stony, and he was holding Angel's arm tightly. His face was close to hers. She looked frightened, and she was sobbing.

"Leave her alone," I said. I spoke slowly and forcefully but without yelling. "You aren't the boss of her."

"Yes I am!" he growled. He leaned down and stuck his face close to mine. I planted my feet solidly on the floor and didn't move. My hands were fists by my side, and my heart was pumping hard. "She'll do whatever I say, whenever I say it. You understand, you little crooked-toothed brat? She's mine."

"No she isn't. She's her own person." I spat the words at him. "She can make her own decisions."

"Leave Lacey alone, Kelvin. She has nothing to do with this," said Angel, but her words sounded weak. She was still crying and rubbing her arm where he had gripped her. "Just go, Kelvin. Go now."

He glared at Angel, then jerked his head at me. "Stay out of this!" he said, pointing his index finger at me. It was black on the tip. "Or else!" He slammed the door so hard the walls shook. I ran down the stairs and locked the door.

Angel and I fell into each other's arms. We both sobbed.

"Angel, you have to do something. You can't be afraid all the time. It's wrong. You need someone loving, like Dad, not someone who is always going to be scaring you."

"But..." She sobbed harder. "But that's what I told him. I told him I wouldn't move in with his family. I said I needed to stay here."

"And that's how he acted? He's dangerous, Angel. You have to tell Mum and Dad."

"But I have Kayden to think about. He's her father."

"You want Kayden to grow up with him? What if he starts yelling at her or...or hitting her?"

"I know," she whimpered. "I know you're right."

We sat together in the hallway, with the whole sides of our bodies touching. Angel reached for my hand, and with her other hand started wiping away tears. "There's more," she said quietly. "The police questioned Kelvin today." She started to cry little jerky cries that stuck in her throat. "They think he's the one who broke the church windows and your flowerpots and wrote those words and everything. I'm so ashamed, and I'm so worried about what will happen." She lifted the bottom of her shirt to wipe her face. "He'll probably go to jail this time. He says he didn't do it, that he was set up. I want to believe him. I really do. He is good inside, better than people think, better than you think. But still, I'm not so sure about this... I don't know whether to believe him or not. Whatever I say, or whatever questions I ask just seem to make things worse."

That was when I remembered his finger pointing at me. The black on his fingertip. Was it grease? Or was it paint? Black paint from a spray can? Paint that wouldn't wash off?

I put my arms around my big sister and held her again the way our mother used to. I wanted to tell her about the paint on his finger, how someone using spray paint would get it on their forefinger if they weren't careful, but she didn't need to feel any sadder than she already felt. I felt sad for her and for my flowers and for the church windows. I wanted to cry, too. "It's OK," I said. "It's OK. Everything will be all right." But I didn't see how anything would be OK ever again.

My flowers were dead. Kelvin would go to jail. Angel would be sad, and Kayden wouldn't have a father.

I wished my father was at home. Dad would know what to do.

*Chapter 16*

# Two Days!

When Dad came home, he and Mum agreed that Angel needed to stay with us. Dad said that Kelvin wasn't grown up enough yet to look after a family. He said Kelvin needed to finish school and prove himself worthy before he could think of stealing away *his* daughter. That made me feel a lot better, and I think it made Angel feel a lot better.

Sewing is a breeze now. I've been sewing nearly every day for more than a month, and instead of making just basic tote bags, I have started to branch out. I remembered the drawings Angel had made of purses, and I cut pieces of fabric to follow her designs. I made swimming bags with pieces of cord for straps, and fancy purses with curved flaps and fringes. One of my best ones had a brown and white pattern with a long fringe that danced when you touched it.

I sewed every night, not just because the African grandmothers needed help, but because I discovered that I loved sewing. I was worried that I would run out of material, but it seemed that every time my supply ran low, someone heard about what I was doing and donated something: fabric, thread, buttons, beads, tassels, and fringes. Mrs. Martinez, Mrs. Buchanan, and

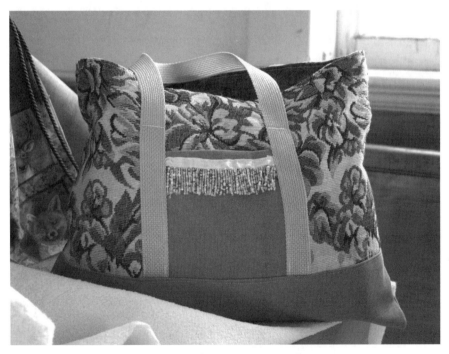

Soon basic tote bags were made unique
by adding pockets and decorative trim.

Shoulder straps had to be pinned carefully,
but made the bags look different.

Lila seemed to be best at spreading the news. Every time I saw them, they gave me new things. Even people from Strathmore had heard about what I was doing and had started sending odds and ends. Sometimes they were big pieces of fabric and sometimes just scraps and bits that I could match up with another piece to make a purse. One of the boys at Sequoia brought in long, narrow scraps of leather that his grandmother had given him. We braided three of them together, and he sewed the ends onto a purse to make a shoulder strap. He also took a piece and snipped it evenly along the short edge to make a fringe. I sewed that piece onto the flap of the same purse. Another boy had an idea to make strings of beads to decorate the sides of some tote bags, so we tried that, too.

Usually I sewed on the machine at home, and did the hand-sewing of buttons and fringes and toggles when I went to Sequoia after school. It helped that Dad was home more often now and that Mum was pretty much back to normal. I had less housework to do and more time to sew, sew, sew.

I just wished it was brighter inside the church basement. It's hard to sew without the proper light. Two of the windows were still boarded up, so it was fairly dark inside, even when it was bright and sunny outside. Workers with a big window on the side of their truck were outside the church and working with power tools to replace the church window. I hoped it would have

A lot of people – even boys – became interested in the project.

colored glass like the old one. I didn't know what they were going to do about the awful words written on the side of the church. Some of the boys had scrubbed at the words with cleaners and wire brushes, but they hadn't come off. I hoped the words wouldn't be there forever to remind me about what had happened to my plants.

A few of the girls at Sequoia were becoming interested in what I was doing. I had shown some girls how to do fancy embroidery stitches and some hand-sewing. Some of the girls – and the guys – were interested in learning how to use a sewing machine, so Mrs. B. said she would try to get one or two for the school. She said I could help teach the class, which was exciting.

She was also going to ask my dad to help. She said he would be a good role model for the boys.

I was hand-sewing the diamond pattern I'd beaded with Kahasi onto a purse when Trisha asked, "Can you make something for me? Come on, I need a bag to carry things now that I have a baby." She'd had her baby three weeks before, a little boy with hair so black and thick that it looked like fur.

I told her I couldn't make something for her because I was making purses for African grandmothers.

"Why do African grandmothers need purses? I need a purse. I don't think *they* need them," she said.

"Come on, Trisha. You know I'm going to sell them," I said. "When I get enough finished, Mrs. B. is going to take them to Calgary and give them to the Grandmothers to Grandmothers group there. They'll sell them and send the money to Africa to help the children. So, if you want one, you have to buy it."

"But I don't have any money to buy one. This one is really nice," she said, picking up the tote bag with the big sunflowers on the sides and bottom. She put it on her shoulder and walked around. "I like this one, but it should have a pocket on the outside," she said, putting it down and picking up another one. "Oooo, this one is *nice*."

"That one's not done yet," I said. She had picked up one made of soft blue corduroy. "That sparkly part is just pinned on, so be careful." She held it up to the light and moved it back and forth so it would sparkle.

"I could show you how to sew," I offered. "Maybe you could help me, and I could help you, and we could both help the grandmothers."

Trisha glanced over at Mrs. B.'s desk, then she picked up a needle and snipped a piece of blue thread from the spool. "OK, what do I do?" she said, trying to fit the thread into the eye of the needle. I showed her how to wet the end of the thread before threading the needle, and how to roll the thread in her fingers to make a knot in the end.

"You can work on that applique if you want – the bird-shaped one you like so much." She picked up the blue purse, and I taught her how to make the running stitch that Kahasi had first shown me. "Small stitches," I said, just the way my grandmother had. "The smaller the better."

Trisha stuck out her tongue a little as she concentrated on making a line of stitches along the side of the sparkly bird. She was slow, but her sewing was neat and surprisingly straight.

"Trish-a..." Mrs. B. called. She said her name very slowly, so Trisha knew to move fast.

"I've got to go. I'm supposed to be doing something else. I'll finish this tomorrow, OK?" she whispered.

I nodded and went to pick up one of the babies, who needed

his diaper changed. When I came out of the bathroom, Mrs. B. was talking on the phone and looking straight at me. As soon as she hung up, she said, "Lacey, you will never believe this! The grandmothers are coming. They are coming here! To Gleichen! To Sequoia!"

"You mean the African grandmothers? They are going to come all the way here?"

"Yes! Yes! Yes!" she said. She had jumped up from her desk and was bouncing up and down like a little kid. "Two of the African grandmothers are in Canada right now. They are here promoting the Grandmothers to Grandmothers campaign, telling people about it and trying to get more support. It turns out they have an extra day, and rather than go to Banff or Jasper or anywhere else for a little holiday, they want to come here. They want to meet you!"

"Me? But I...I've hardly done anything yet. I...well...I...I guess it would be nice to meet them. But I..." I put the baby back in the playpen with some toys and picked up the blue purse. All these piles of fabric and buttons made me want to keep on sewing and never stop.

"Maybe we can have a party," she said. "Yes, of course we'll have a party. Oh my, we have so much to do."

"Don't worry," I said. "The grandmothers must be very busy. It will take them a long time to get here."

"No, they are in Calgary right now. They will be here in just two days!"

"Two days?" I couldn't believe what I was hearing. "Two days is not enough time."

"It may not be enough, but it's all that we have," said Mrs. B. "Let's see. We'll get the school tepee set up, and we'll have to invite the elders. Oh, and some of the people from the school board. We'll have to have food, lots of food..." She went on talking but I wasn't listening.

The elders taught the boys how to set up the school's tepee.

I wasn't worried about food or the tepee or guests. I had a much bigger problem.

How was I going to make enough purses for the grandmothers in just two days?

Chapter 17

# Help!

"That one next," I said, pointing. "Use this pattern. Angel, I need that silvery thread. Hurry up! We can't waste time." I felt like an army sergeant ordering my mother and my big sister around, but it felt good to have the help. The pile of purses beside Angel kept growing. My mum cut out the patterns, I sewed, Angel trimmed the threads and ironed the seams, and Dad added buttons and snaps. Trisha had stopped in for a little while to help, but her baby was fussing and cranky, so she took him home. A few other people stopped by, too, because they had heard about the African grandmothers coming and were curious to see what was happening. I wouldn't let anyone talk very long. I'd just say, "Hi," and "Could you sew on that button?" or "Can you check that that zipper works properly?" or "Can you spread out that material on the counter for Mum?" I kept putting people to work. We needed all the help we could get, even if it was just for five or ten minutes each. But mostly, it was just me and my family that night.

"Isn't this enough, Lacey?" Angel whined.

"How many are finished?"

"Twelve," she counted. "I'm tired. Can't twelve be enough?"

I looked at the clock on the stove. Almost ten – way past my bedtime. I hoped my mum and dad wouldn't notice. "We have to keep going," I insisted.

Angel pouted, but she didn't put down the scissors. Fabric that people had given me was spread all over the kitchen counter, the table, and the coffee table from the living room. Kahasi was sitting in a comfortable chair we had moved into the doorway, half in the kitchen and half in the hall. She was helping with the detail work, sewing on appliques and buttons and braiding shoulder straps. She did all this nearly at the same time as she was beading little crosses. For someone old, she could sure do a lot of things. The Siksika grandmothers were making rosaries with beaded crosses to give to the African grandmothers. They would be a sign of love from the Siksika grandmothers. "I don't want to let anyone down," I said. "Look at all this beautiful material. How would you feel if you gave me material to make

Twenty-seven purses were finished by the time
the late-night sewing session ended.

purses, and then, on the day of the sale, you couldn't find any made from your material? Besides, the more we make, the more we can sell. And the more we can sell, the more money we can give to the African grandmothers."

Angel sighed loudly. "Yah, yah, I know. The grandmothers need our help, but how many will be enough?"

I looked at Mum. "I've only got until tomorrow. I'd like to keep going until I'm too tired to make the stitches straight or until I run out of material." Angel groaned dramatically. "Am I allowed to Mum? Can I stay up late?" I wished the sewing machine was quieter when it sewed. I wished I were invisible.

But I don't think Mum heard my question. She was too busy concentrating on the cutting.

A wrestling match was going on in the living room, and Dad had put down his sewing to play. "Ladies and gentlemen, it's the Elimination Chamber," he said in a loud announcer's voice. "Look out, crowd. Here comes...the Term-in-a-tor!" He threw away his pretend microphone and jumped into the middle of the boys who were sprawled and play-fighting all over the living room. They'd keep at it until someone was crying, and then Dad would send the younger ones to bed. We were all allowed to stay up late because no one was going to school tomorrow. Everyone was coming to the celebration for the African grandmothers.

Finally, my mum answered me, nodding ever so slightly, a tired smile crossing her face. "Yes, you may stay up late, but maybe not as late as you want," she said. She didn't mention that we'd been sewing almost nonstop for nearly six hours.

Neither she nor Kahasi could help with the machine sewing, because they didn't know how, but Mum turned out to be swift and accurate with a pair of scissors, and Kahasi just kept on and on at the detail work, as if she were a machine. With every seam I sewed, I thought about those African grandmothers and their dying children. Staying up late and sewing was easy compared to having family members pass on, especially if they passed away young.

"You'll be there, Kahasi, won't you?" I asked.

My sister rolled her eyes as if it was a stupid question.

"I don't know," said Kahasi. "I'd like to see how these women look, but it might be too many people there for me. Besides, me, I don't know what I would say to someone from Africa."

"I think you'd say, 'Hello, I'm glad to meet you.'"

She chuckled her soft laugh. "Yes, I suppose that would be a good place to start."

It was as dark as a cave outside when I looked out the window. Not even the moon was shining. I blinked my eyes slowly. They felt full of sand. My eyes were begging me to sleep, but my mind said to keep going.

"Lacey, my girl, I think it's time," Mum said, laying both her hands gently on my shoulders.

"How many?" I asked. We counted the purses as we put them in a big plastic bin.

"Twenty-seven," Mum said. "Twenty-seven! I can't believe it." She smiled, and I smiled too. In my mind, I added the twenty-seven, plus the ones I'd made in the past few weeks, and the one I still had to finish. There'd probably be a good selection, and if people bought them, I could probably make a couple of hundred dollars for the African grandmothers. I was snipping the threads of the last one – number twenty-eight – and thinking about what the African grandmothers might buy with the money, when Mum took it from my hands and dropped it in the bin. "Twenty eight," she said. "I think twenty-eight is the right amount for one girl and one mother and one sister and one old grandmother to make. You need to get some sleep. Tomorrow is a big day, and you'll need to catch the early bus."

"But can't I just finish..."

"No," Mum said. "It's time for bed."

I stumbled down the hallway to my pink bedroom. I didn't stop at the bathroom to brush my teeth, and I didn't bother with my nightdress. I just crawled into bed wearing all my daytime clothes. I hoped my teeth wouldn't rot during the night, but I was willing to take the chance.

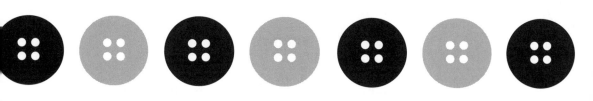

## Chapter 18

# Kelvin Speaks Up

"What do you mean, I can't take this on the bus?" I asked Cheryl, the school bus driver. "I have to take this to school. It's really important."

"No, it's too big. It's against regulations. There's no place to put it. You're not allowed to block the aisle and it's too big to put under the seat."

"I can put it on the seat beside me, and the sewing machine under the seat," I said, lifting the bin with the twenty-eight purses onto the bus.

"We'd have to leave someone behind. There wouldn't be enough room, Lacey."

I looked at my sister yawning at the bottom of the bus steps.

She had Kayden in her arms and the sewing machine in its case by her feet. "Angel will stay behind and catch the later bus," I offered. "That leaves one seat empty, plus Kayden's car seat space. So then there's enough room."

Cheryl looked down at Angel. "That OK with you?"

"Sure," Angel said, yawning again. "I had a late night. Too bad I didn't know before I got out of bed."

I beamed at Angel. "Thank you! I'll make it up to you," I promised, as I took the sewing machine from her.

Unusual things were already happening by the time Cheryl dropped me off at Sequoia. A television crew was there, and a reporter introduced himself. The reporters all wanted to talk to me, but there was still work to be done. While TV people were setting up cameras, the boys from Sequoia were rearranging the church pews. They even set up a table for the sewing machine.

"Can you set up some tables for a display, too?" I asked. "I have a lot of purses I'd like to show." I left the sewing machine and the purses on the table and ran downstairs to help Mrs. B. and Lila with the feast. Two of the reporters followed me and took pictures of me and the other people helping. They asked everybody questions while we chopped vegetables and mixed frozen juice.

Mrs. B. was stirring a huge pot of chili on the stove, and Lila was talking quickly, firing off commands to everyone within earshot. "Lacey, peel those carrots and cut them into sticks," she said, as soon as she saw me. "Trisha, get back here. This lettuce needs to be torn into smaller pieces. Think bite-size. Where are those boys? We need set-up down here, too.

"Come on! Hurry up! *Eh stu!* They'll be here soon, and we have to be ready."

Everyone pitched in to help prepare for the celebration.

I smiled as I cut the carrots and watermelon. Lila sounded as bossy as I had sounded last night. I felt so excited that the African grandmothers were coming that I wasn't even tired from staying up late. I couldn't believe they were really coming. I never thought it would turn out like this. I just thought I could raise a little money to help them, and now they would be here, in real life. Mrs. B. told me they had never been to a small place in Canada before. They had been only to big cities like Calgary and Toronto. It would be such an honor to meet them. This was going to be my best day ever.

I was nearly finished the chopping when Kelvin came in. Even though we were almost related, I still didn't want to look at him. No matter how nice he was being lately, I was still mad about how he wrecked my flowers and about how he treated Angel. He came close beside me and touched my arm lightly. "Come. Follow me," he said quietly. When I hesitated, he took my hand gently, like a brother. "I want to show you something," he said.

I followed him up the main stairs and outside the church. He led me past the brand new basement windows and the wall that had been freshly painted to cover up the bad words. He led me to the back of the school, where the elders had told the boys how to set up the school's tepee. There was a flowerpot overflowing with large pink flowers and delicate blue and white ones hanging from the fence, and on the ground near the entrance to the tepee was a clump of sweet grass with its purplish spring flowers. Other native plants, such as pale purple crocuses and clumps of wild chives with ball-like purple flowers were planted around the fence. The plants were even prettier than the ones that he had wrecked. Kelvin didn't say anything. He just stood there and looked down, showing his respect for me.

"You? You did this?"

His black hair fell over his face when he nodded. "I had help," he said.

"Kelvin? You?" I asked again, in disbelief. He nodded again. "But how?"

"The old lady who has that big garden, the one who brings vegetables to Sequoia? I fixed her car the other day. She wanted to give me twenty bucks. I didn't want any money, but since she had a lot of nice flowers, I asked if I could have a few of them instead. She gave me that big pot full of flowers," he said, nodding towards the pot hanging on the fence. "This other stuff, me and the guys just dug up and stuck in the dirt. I don't know if they'll live, but if they get enough water, maybe they will. They might even come back again next year, too, without planting them over again." He spoke slowly, and mostly kept his head down and scuffed his shoe back and forth in the grass. He looked embarrassed, rather than proud, of what he'd done.

I didn't know what to say. There were so many thoughts in my head. Kelvin had done something good? It couldn't be. It had to be a trick. He must want something. Then I remembered my grandmother's voice saying that sometimes thinking with your head makes you mixed up. She had told me to listen to my heart. I also remembered her telling me about the white buffalo calf and how it would bring a time of peace and harmony. Was the legend true?

Kelvin lifted his head and looked at me. The hair fell from his eyes without that proud flick he liked to do. His eyes weren't hard and angry – they were as gentle as Angel's.

"We have to get along, Lacey. We're family."

But he was my enemy. The one who yelled at my sister and bullied her, the one who pointed his finger at me and told me to stay out of things. Replacing the plants he had destroyed wouldn't change that. He would still be mean, still be a bully.

"I know you think I smashed your flowerpots, but I didn't. The police don't believe me either. No one believes me – no one except Angel. But I didn't do it, and that's the truth," he said. "Ever since I stole that car, everyone is against me. They finger me every time anything happens. They want to prove I'm just like my father, but I'm not. I'm a different person."

"But if you didn't wreck them, why did you..."

"I did it for you and for Angel." He looked down at the

ground again. "I wanted to make something pretty, something good."

I just stood there looking at the flowers and not really believing that Kelvin could do this.

"It's like your dad told me. I have to prove myself, in small ways, then in big ways. Over and over, he said. He said I'd have to keep doing good things, and doing good things until people started believing in me, trusting me." He scuffed the grass some more. "I'm trying, you know? Because I want to be a good partner for Angel and a good father for Kayden. Sometimes I still get it wrong, but I'm trying to be a better person. Step by step, you know?"

"But your finger was all black, and you were mad that you failed math..." I looked at his hands, a mix of grease from working at the garage and dirt from planting. Could I have been wrong? Had it been dried grease and not paint on his finger that day?

"It wasn't me," he said. I stood quietly looking at him, and my heart understood.

"I believe you," I said, then I put my arms around him and hugged him like a brother. He hugged me back, but just for a second.

"It's the white buffalo calf," I said quietly, letting the words in my mind come out. "It's just like Kahasi said."

Kelvin squinted his eyes at me. "You mean that white buffalo at the zoo?"

I nodded. "Kahasi told me how it's a sacred animal,"

"I know about that. Mrs. B. is getting a bus or a big van to take whoever wants to go to see it. Maybe you could go, too."

"Really? There's a bus going to the zoo?" I wanted to go, but even more, I wanted Kahasi to go. Maybe I could get her on that bus.

## Chapter 19

# Florence and Zubeda

"They're here! They're here!" Trisha called into the church. "Hurry, Lacey. They're here!"

I looked up at the hands of the clock. "Eleven o'clock. Right on time," I murmured. I was inside sewing one last tote bag, while people wandered into the church. I was nearly finished; I just had to sew on some fringe or buttons to dress it up. I stood up, brushed away the bits of thread, and ran my hands over my head to smooth my hair. The pews were filling with people chattering excitedly, as if they were at a wedding. Most of the faces were of people I knew.

"Lacey! The van is pulling up. Come on!" pleaded Trisha.

By the time I walked to the back of the church, my heart

The African grandmothers were named Florence and Zubeda.

was drowning out the sounds of children laughing and crying. Butterflies were dancing in my stomach as I watched the shiny black van roll towards the school and stop. The back door opened, and a woman unfolded from the van. My drumming heart pushed me down the steps towards her as another woman and a man got out. Their smiles were as big as the sky.

The skin of the first woman was as dark as the soil beneath the prairie grasses. I had never seen anyone with skin so dark. I wanted to look more at her, but it would be disrespectful. Instead, I hung my head and looked at her feet.

"Lacey Little Bird!" the woman said. She put her hand gently under my chin and lifted my face. The inner part of her hand was as pink as a newborn rabbit.

"It is OK to look at me," she said in English, "and I want to look at you." Slowly I lifted my brown eyes to look into her brown eyes. "My name is Florence," she added.

Florence looked like a bright tropical bird wearing glasses. She had a pink and pale purple scarf twisted around her head, so I couldn't see her hair. Her dress matched the scarf and had a long pink skirt like the kind Kahasi wears when she wants to be fancy. Her jacket looked like a leopard, and her purse was large and white.

"I want to say thank you," she told me. Her hand moved from my chin to the top of my back as she pulled me into a huge hug and squeezed me so tightly that our hearts were together, both beating fast. She held me for a long time like that.

She spoke in English, but the words sounded somehow different; they were slow and careful and correct. She spoke softly, like a Siksika elder, but her words still sounded strange to my ears.

I could feel my mouth move into a smile that reflected hers, and I knew she could see my crooked teeth, and even the holes where new teeth were still growing. Behind me I could hear the church door opening and the older kids and their children coming out for a look. Florence looked up, and her face glowed with happiness. "We have a welcoming party, I see. It is the same in my village. Everyone wants to take part."

She beckoned for the other grandmother to join us, and she pulled me into a tight hug.

"We are going to have a celebration – to show you about our people," I said.

The other African grandmother was named Zubeda. She looked younger, and her straight black hair was dyed with pink streaks on the top. She wore a long, flowing skirt, too, and a red wool jacket. She had a silver camera looped around her wrist.

"Lacey, will you be inviting our guests in?" asked Mrs. Buchanan.

I nodded and took Florence's warm hand and led her up the steps.

Chapter 20

# The Best Day Ever

The upstairs of the church was overflowing when we walked in. I don't know where so many people could have come from. People were sitting in the pews and standing along the sides. I saw many Siksika elders, and also people I didn't know, who must have been from the city. I waved to my mother and father, who were standing at the back with Angel. Kayden was in her arms and Kelvin was beside her. My brothers were all there, lined up against the wall. I also found Auntie Michelle and Uncle Douglas, but I couldn't find Kahasi. I didn't see her anywhere. But then I heard her voice. She was sitting behind me, using her hands to talk to some people I hadn't seen before. I gave a little wave to Mrs. Martinez, too.

Although some of the styles were similar, each purse was unique.

Someone had set up a huge display of purses all across the front of the church, on tables and hanging on the walls in the place where the minister usually stands. Whoever made the display had done a good job; you could see all the different colors and shapes. Two wool blankets were stretched out along the front of the church; they would be gifts for the African grandmothers.

We asked the grandmothers and the man to sit in the front row of the church. I sat on the left side, where the boys had set up the sewing machine.

Mrs. B. welcomed everyone, and then she surprised me by saying, "And now, Lacey, could you say a few words?"

Me? What was I going to say? I walked nervously to the front and took the microphone from her. "Umm," I said, "I didn't think it would be this big." Some people laughed softly, so I laughed a little bit too. I reminded myself that these people were mostly my friends and family.

"I can't actually believe this is happening, that it's all real," I said. "When I started making purses, I just wanted to try to help a little. I never for one second thought I'd get to meet any African grandmothers." I said thank you to the grandmothers for coming all the way across the ocean, and to Kahasi for teaching me to sew in the first place, and to my family and the kids from Sequoia who had helped me. Then I said thank you to everyone for coming, and I handed the microphone back to Mrs. B. My hands were shaking, and my legs felt like jelly. I took two steps towards my seat when I remembered something. Mrs. B. looked surprised when I went up and stood beside her again. I whispered, "I have one more thing to say," so she held the microphone toward me. "I almost forgot. Thanks to everyone who came to my house last night to help. I'm sorry if I was so bossy." I noticed a lot of heads nodding and people laughing softly.

A boy from Sequoia played his guitar and sang a song of thanks he had made for the grandmothers. Another boy played a drum while a girl performed a jingle dance, wearing the dress Kahasi and I had sewn together last year. The rows of tiny bells – which were really the tops of olden-days tobacco cans – tinkled grandly with each step she took. Her steps were so light that her feet hardly seemed to touch the floor.

Other performers wore costumes with bright blue feathers to dance the chicken dance and the grass dance. Then it was time for Florence and Zubeda to speak. They told us about Kenya, their country in Africa, and about the fifty grandchildren with no mothers that they look after.

"Africa has become a continent of orphans," Florence said. "We have lost a generation. Already, about thirteen million children in Africa have no parents. It is because of the disease AIDS that the parents are dying. Imagine all of the children in Canada without parents. Now, you can imagine a place without a generation. Now, you can imagine Africa.

"We are the grandmothers. We bury our children, but there is no time to grieve. No time to cry. We have work to do. We must help our children's children survive and become strong.

People from Siksika demonstrated parts of the
Blackfoot culture by singing and dancing.

The African grandmothers were given
wool blankets as a sign of respect.

"In some of the forty-seven countries south of the Sahara Desert in Africa, half the orphans live in families headed by their grandmothers. We must look after the babies, the little ones, and the teenagers who are left behind." Florence handed the microphone to Zubeda.

"It should not be this way," Zubeda continued. "But we do the best we can do. That is all we can do. We give our thanks to the grandmothers in Canada – to young women like Lacey – who understand our pain and want to help us. We understand hardship and loss, and I think that you understand, too."

The Siksika elders and some people from Sequoia did a robing ceremony with Florence and Zubeda, draping each of them with a wool blanket. It's a Blackfoot tradition that shows honor and acceptance. The blankets show that the grandmothers are held in high esteem. Other people gave them traditional gifts of sage, sweet grass, and feathers. Wrapped in their blankets, Zubeda and Florence sang us a lullaby that they sing to the children without mothers and aunties.

After the formal part with the singing and dancing, came the best part. It was time for the Siksika grandmothers and the African grandmothers to meet face to face. They gathered each other in their arms and hugged tightly. They hugged as if they would never let go. It was as if they were long-ago sisters who hadn't seen each other in a long, long time.

The African grandmothers and the Siksika grandmothers exchanged gifts. It was as if they were long-ago sisters.

I watched Kahasi take Zubeda in her arms. It was the longest hug I had ever seen, and when Kahasi pulled away, she wiped tears from her eyes. Zubeda had tears, too. I don't know if the tears were of joy or sadness.

After all the hugging, the grandmothers gathered in a circle to exchange presents. It was funny to watch them like that – black and silver and gray and pink heads together. They chattered like a bunch of ravens arguing over who would go first. It was as if they were talking all at the same time, yet they could all hear and understand each other. Every once in a while one would lift her head, and you would see the big smile lighting up her face.

I couldn't see Lila, but even above the sound of the grandmothers, I could hear her. She was talking to everyone and selling purses to the people who had money. Mostly it was people from Strathmore and Calgary who were buying the things I had made. I hoped they had brought a lot of money.

It was so noisy in the church that I didn't think anyone would mind if I turned on the sewing machine. As I sewed, I watched the grandmothers with their heads together, making sounds of laughter and little whoops of happiness as they talked. One of the Siksika grandmothers sounded like one of those dolls you squeeze to make it giggle. It was the kind of laughter that makes you smile to yourself even if you don't know the joke. I felt so full of joy as I sewed. It felt so good to help them in my small way and to have all the grandmothers together.

Mrs. Martinez came to see me. The brown purse with the fringe was hanging from her shoulder. "Do you see the one I bought?" I smiled up at her. "You have made some beautiful ones, but this one is my favorite. I love how this fringe moves," she said.

Then Zubeda left the group of grandmothers to come visit me. She had the red blanket around her shoulders and a rosary around her neck as if it were a necklace. She gave me a beaded pin of a gray-haired grandmother holding a baby. She pinned it onto my sweater and told me she liked my pink hoop earrings. She said pink was her favorite color, too.

I knew that the pin was a gift I would keep always, to remember this day. The beads were the same as the ones I used, and the beading seemed to be done the same way Kahasi had taught me. How strange it was, I thought, that African people and Siksika people would bead the same way, though they lived almost a whole world apart. We are different in where we stay, and how we look, but inside, I think we are the same.

Chapter 21

# Kitamatsinopowa

After everyone ate as much as they wanted, the Siksika grandmothers, the African grandmothers, and some of the rest of us drove in vans to Blackfoot Crossing. Zubeda held my hand as we walked along the trails by the historical center that's built into the side of the coulee. We started down the wide trail that leads to the trees and the river.

"You can see my house from here," I said, pointing to the right. "If you count, it's one, two, three, four. You see?"

"Yes, I see it," said Zubeda. "It looks like a good house, and very big. You stay warm there even when it is so cold?" She was wearing wool socks inside her sandals, a borrowed winter jacket, and her new blanket. I was wearing jeans, my black shirt with

The African grandmothers were taken on a tour along the trails
at the Blackfoot Crossing Historical Centre.

*Kitamatsinopowa*

The African grandmothers said that Siksika reminded
them of their home in Kenya, except that Siksika didn't
have any noisy monkeys.

the ruffles at the shoulders, and a sweater. It was a warm spring day with a lot of sunshine.

"Oh, yes," I said. "It keeps us very warm – even in the winter, when the wind blows and there is snow."

She looked all around and smiled her ray-of-sunshine smile. "I have never seen snow," she said, then paused. "It is just like Kenya here – the hills, the trees." She pulled her blanket closer around the winter jacket and gazed at the land. "It is like being at home again. Even your people are the same as my people. It is the same, all of it, except for the cold. I have never been so cold before."

I didn't know that Alberta looked like Africa. I wondered how it would be to have an elephant come out from the trees. Or a monkey.

Zubeda stopped walking abruptly and looked into my eyes. Her voice was almost a whisper as she spoke. "Something is wrong. Ah, I know what is different. It's too quiet."

"It's quiet here because we are a long way from the city. The city is very noisy."

"No, no," she said. "The animals. The monkeys. I can't hear the monkeys. Why are they so silent?"

"We don't have monkeys here. It's too cold for them. We keep our monkeys in the zoo."

Her mouth fell open, and she looked frightened at the idea

Lisa Jo pointed out her house in South Camp.

of keeping monkeys in the zoo. "It's better for them there," I added quickly. "They couldn't live here. It's too cold, and the trees probably don't have the right kind of food."

Zubeda shook her head slowly in disbelief. "My, my. What a waste of perfectly good trees. You should have monkeys. I think they would like these trees." She laughed. "Maybe you could give them blankets and big socks to stay warm."

I felt both sad and happy when it was time for the African grand-mothers to go. I was happy that I had met some of the people I would be helping, but sad that they had to leave me. I also felt as if I had grown taller, and my heart felt different inside my body as I stood on the sidewalk and waved goodbye. I also thought of the journey I hoped Kahasi would soon make to Calgary to see the white buffalo calf.

I went back inside the church after the van pulled away. Most of the guests had returned to Siksika, Calgary, and Strathmore. The church was quiet now, as it usually is, but Lila was still there. She was tidying up the display of the purses.

"I was very proud of you today, Lacey," she said.

I smiled my thanks and slumped onto one of the wooden church seats. I was tired from sewing late into the night, and from the excitement of the day, but part of me wanted to go to the machine in the corner and keep on making purses. "Did you sell very many?" I asked.

"We sold lots and lots. So far, I've counted over a thousand dollars in the cash box."

"A *thousand* dollars?" I couldn't believe it. There were still lots of purses on the tables.

"Uh-huh. And I think we'll sell more. Mrs. B. and I thought we would leave the display here for a few days. Some people who couldn't come today might want to buy something. A thousand dollars is pretty amazing, isn't it?"

What was even more amazing was that Lila talked people into buying another eight hundred dollars worth of purses in the next two days. I never knew one girl could make that much money. But I also knew that one girl couldn't stop now. I had to keep on sewing for the faraway grandmothers.

I didn't get to go to see the white buffalo calf with Kahasi, but Angel did. And Kelvin. Angel said that when our grandmother saw that animal grazing at the zoo, she just stood at the railing as if she had been turned into stone. She closed her eyes and stood there as still as could be and didn't say a thing. When everyone wanted to look at the other animals, she said she would just stay there on a bench, and they could come get her when it was time to go. Kelvin stayed with her. Kahasi told me she felt connected to the white buffalo calf in a way she couldn't explain, that it made her feel peaceful in a way she had never felt before.

Kahasi has a lot of old legends and sayings that she teaches me from time to time. One of my favorites is the one about pebbles in the water. She once told me that everything we do is like throwing a pebble into still water – that a small circle makes a bigger circle, then a bigger one, until the circles are so big that they don't touch anymore – but still, they are all connected to that pebble.

When I think back to those curled-up seeds and the flowers that grew, learning to sew, the purses, and the African grandmothers visiting, the coming of the white buffalo calf, and Kelvin wanting to change his future, I know what she says is true: Everything is connected. Everything is a circle.

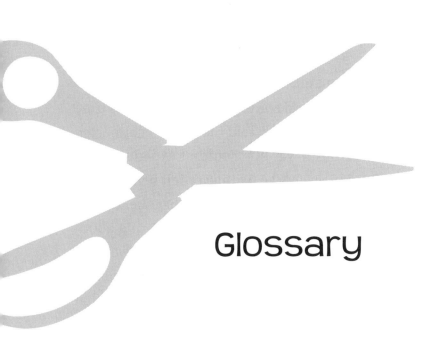

# Glossary

**AIDS:** Acquired Immune Deficiency Syndrome, a deadly infectious disease.

**Blackfoot Confederacy:** The five First Nations: the Kainai, the Piikani, the Siksika, the Nakoda, and the Tsuu T'ina.

**Eh stu:** Blackfoot for "Hurry up! Right now!"

**Fry Bread:** A quickbread, made from flour, water, and baking powder, that is deep-fried.

**Immistsiihkiitaan:** Blackfoot for fry bread.

**Kahasi:** Blackfoot word for "my grandmother."

**Kitamatsinopowa:** Blackfoot for "Farewell." Literally, "I'll see you on the trail."

**Matsowa'p:** Blackfoot for beautiful.

**Napikwan:** Blackfoot name for white people.

**Ookonooki:** Blackfoot for saskatoon berries, sweet purplish berries that grow on trees.

**Siksika:** Blackfoot name for Blackfoot people. Also, a First Nations community about 100 km (65 miles) east of Calgary, Alberta.

**Sipaattsimaan:** Blackfoot word for sweet grass.

**Smudge:** A purification ceremony in which sweet grass, and sometimes sage, is burned.

# Afterword

Lisa Jo was a teenager when she started working with the Grandmothers to Grandmothers campaign in the fall of 2006. She has raised more than six thousand dollars to help the African grandmothers, and has inspired others at Sequoia to sew purses too. The purses they make are added to the sale held each year by the Grandmothers to Grandmothers group in Calgary.

The mother of two young children, Lisa Jo now lives in Calgary where she is studying at Mount Royal College. She plans to work with children and youth.

# Sources

**Gleichen, Alberta**
www.gleichenalberta.ca

**Glenbow Museum**
www.glenbow.org/blackfoot
(Blackfoot online, interactive exhibition)

**Grandmothers to Grandmothers program**
www.stephenlewisfoundation.org/grandmothers.htm

**Legend of White Buffalo Calf Woman**
www.merceronline/Native/native05.htm
www.kstrom.net/isk/arvol/buffpipe.html
www.crystalinks.com/buffalocalfwoman.html

**Siksika First Nation**
www.siksikanation.com
www.blackfootcrossing.ca

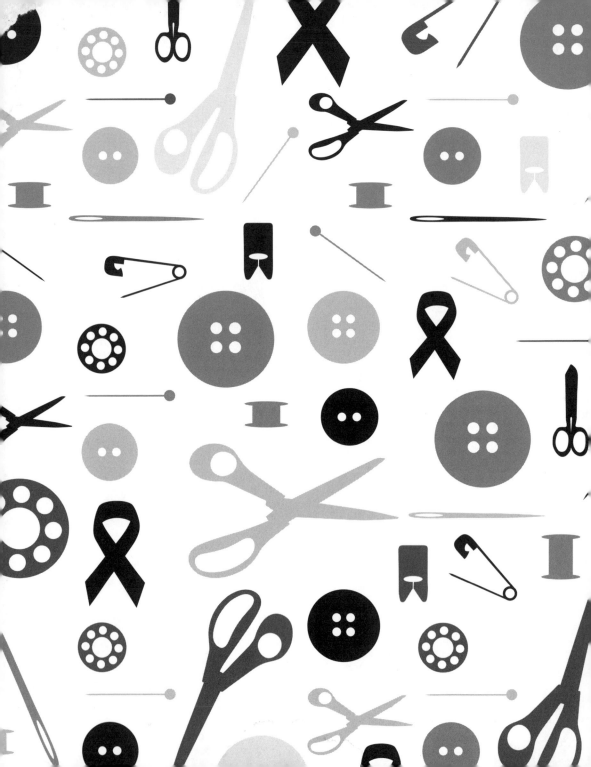